Son of Nobody

ALSO BY Yann Martel

The High Mountains of Portugal

101 Letters to a Prime Minister

Beatrice and Virgil

Life of Pi

Self

The Facts Behind the Helsinki Roccamatios

Son of Nobody

Yann Martel

CANONGATE

First published in Great Britain in 2026
by Canongate Books Ltd, 14 High Street, Edinburgh EH1 1TE

canongate.co.uk

First published in the USA in 2026 by W.W. Norton & Company, Inc, 500 Fifth Avenue, New York, NY 10110

1

Copyright © Yann Martell, 2026
Illustrations © Kima Lenaghan, 2025

The acknowledgments appear on page 60

The right of Yann Martell to be identified as the
author of this work has been asserted by him in accordance
with the Copyright, Designs and Patents Act 1988

Canongate supports copyright, which exists to encourage creativity by making sure that authors, artists and other creative people can be fairly rewarded for their work. Copyright allows authors control over the use and reproduction of their work. No part of this book may be used or reproduced in any manner for the purpose of training artificial intelligence technologies or systems. Canongate expressly reserves this work from text and data mining (Article 4(3) Directive (EU) 2019/790). By buying books (as well as borrowing them from the library) you are supporting authors and publishers and making new and original work possible.

British Library Cataloguing-in-Publication Data
A catalogue record for this book is available on
request from the British Library

ISBN 978 1 83885 907 7
Export ISBN 978 1 83885 908 4

Book design by Marysarah Quinn

Printed and bound by CPI Group (UK) Ltd, Croydon CR0 4YY

The manufacturer's authorised representative in the EU for product safety is BGC Sustainability & Compliance, 7 avenue du Général Leclerc, Paris 75014 (gpsr@baldwinglobalconsulting.com)

(AUKITZ)

AUTHOR'S NOTE

ONCE THERE was a clay pot and it fell and broke. Once there was a man and he too fell.

Let's start with the first, Helen. A few years back, I came upon the jagged remains of a clay pot. This was at Oxford, where I would be spending a year. As part of my introduction to the Faculty of Classics, I had met the curator of the Classical Greece Collections at the Ashmolean Museum, a fellow Canadian as it happens. She'd invited me to have a peek at the museum's vast trove, of which only a fraction is on public display. And so I made my way to that fine museum one September morning, still bleary-eyed with jet lag, and came to be standing in a windowless, neon-lit room with a table in the centre and walls lined with cabinets of wide, shallow metal drawers.

The curator had time to say, "This is the Antiquities Study Room. Most of the artifacts here date from the Archaic period, that is, from the eighth to the fifth centuries BCE, when—" when her cell phone rang.

She answered and quickly looked worried. "Already?" she said, sounding flustered. "I'll be there in a minute." She hung up and turned to me. "Something's come up." She hesitated, then said, "I'll be back shortly. You don't have to go. Please use the nitrile gloves to handle anything." She pointed to the box of blue rubber gloves on the table. Then she was gone.

I looked around, nonplussed. I was here purely on a social visit. I am—or, rather, *was*—a Homeric scholar, and Homeric scholarship is essentially textual. It's even lighter than that: to start with, it was oral. I know about ancient pottery as much as a Homeric scholar needs to know.

The drawers had thin silver handles that invited my fingers to hook them. I chose a drawer at random, "Attic red-figure". After the slightest resistance, it opened with a gliding smoothness as imperceptible as time itself, its slides clicking quietly as it opened fully—these were deep drawers—revealing broken clay pieces from another age, embedded in white foam and neatly arrayed in rows and columns. Most pieces were decorated with truncated drawings, but some had writing scratched on the glaze. The curator had mentioned the Archaic period. That meant these written-upon potsherds—ostraka, in the jargon of the trade—dated from after the end of that civilizational collapse lasting over three hundred years called the Greek Dark Ages, when clay was starting to capture the living breath of words, the first instances of writing. This was the time when *The Iliad* and *The Odyssey* were written down, the West's very first books, after centuries of word-of-mouth transmission.

I closed the drawer, put on a pair of rubber gloves, and opened another drawer, then another. The contents of each burst into view like a landscape. I searched for ostraka with writing on them, because if old Greek pottery wasn't my specialty, old Greek words were. I had a sound knowledge of Ancient Greek and a dogged talent for deciphering it.

Words appeared, in all the awkward glory of early writing. I felt

I was in a noisy hatchery and these hatchlings were trying to say something as they tumbled over, chirping faintly, featherless wings flapping. I was reminded of you, Helen. In early grade school, you too produced writing like this—your name, stray words, simple sentences—the letters crude, the spelling phonetic.

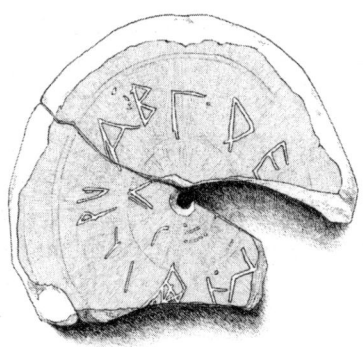

I noticed at the back of one drawer, toward the right, a cluster of six ostraka that were plainly related, looking at the fracture lines. I picked up the largest piece. The letters were quite misshapen. This must be a theta, Θ. Was this a sigma, Σ? I turned it around in my hand. I could make it out now. Backwards? Yes, of course. What about this word? It broke off, but it continued on the next piece, though misspelled; the writer must have meant "because", ENEKA. What were these ostraka saying?

After some effort, I construed the following eight Greek words, all in capital letters, in four crooked, stacked lines:

NEAΘYATNEIMIE

EKAΨOANTOΣ

ΣAEΔIMYOT

OYTINOΣYIOY

There's an irrepressible feeling that comes off the trembly letters of early Archaic Greek writing and sails across the millennia: a giddy, nearly childish enthusiasm. Being the invention of pragmatic dabblers—illiterate Greek traders of the islands and coasts of the eastern Mediterranean who freely retooled a script used by Phoenician traders, none of them trained scribes—it shows a blissful unconcern for rules and conventions, and it goes any which way. I have seen inscriptions whose letters go right to left, left to right, vertically up, vertically down, in a spiral, sideways, and upside down. In many cases, two methods are combined. It's completely nutty and delightful.

One early favoured way of writing was easy for the eye and the finger to follow. The lines I had before me that morning were a perfect example. Translated exactly, they went:

CEBEREHMAI

AUSEOFPSOASOF

NOSAEDIM

OFNOBODY

And with the words separated (a practice adopted much later):

CEB EREH MA I

AUSE OF PSOAS OF

NOS AEDIM

OF NOBODY

This way of writing is called boustrophedon, one of the loveliest words in the English language, from the Greek for "turning like the ox when ploughing", that is, with the text, including the spelling, alternating directions, in this case the first line reading from right to left, the second from left to right, and so on. With boustrophedon, as the eye reaches the end of a line, one can practically hear the clack of the bell and sense the wide blue sky above as the ox comes to the edge of the field and turns to start another furrow, the page an acre of arable land being worked.

I remember when you were learning how to read at school, Helen, you said you felt you were being pushed out of an airplane at the end of every line. You had difficulty landing the parachute of your understanding where it was supposed to, in that tiny field clear across the page. You often landed in another field. In frustration, you rebelled against the diktats of your teacher, and you became very good at it. Whether you were reading a sentence aloud in reverse or turning like the ploughing ox when writing, your nascent literacy made for disjointed narratives that were breathless, freewheeling, and weirdly satisfying. I loved them.

Mrs. Adamson, your grade two teacher, did not. Enough is enough, she decided. This has got to stop. But when a daughter comes home for the second time with a test in which 0/10 is circled in bright red ink and she's in tears, a father has to step up. I marched into Mrs. Adamson's classroom after school one day, an academic tome in my hands.

"She's gone boustrophedon," I explained to her. I showed her photographs of examples from Ancient Greece. "It's the natural way to read and write. Are there line breaks in our minds? No, there are only sinuous furrows of thoughts. As we farm, so we should read and write. The way we do it now, the sentences all chopped up, it's so wrong—why did we ever change?"

Mrs. Adamson, thirty years on the job, looked at me steadily and replied, "I don't know, Mr. Donne. Maybe because we're not in Ancient Greece anymore? Helen can't keep writing like that, zigzagging to and fro down the page. Do you imagine her filling out a job application like that? She won't get the job!"

"Let's not worry about her job prospects just yet. She's seven. She'll get there. It took the Greeks over three hundred years, into the fifth century before Christ, before they agreed on the direction in which they would write. Sadly, they put the ox out to pasture."

Mrs. Adamson rolled her eyes.

Set in the current fashion, the sentence on the ostraka read like this (and come on, let's be honest, doesn't it look like a sentence that's been cut into strips by some syntactical butcher? Where's that dancing sway of the head you get with boustrophedon?):

I AM HERE BEC

AUSE OF PSOAS OF

MIDEA SON

OF NOBODY

I wrote the sentence in the notebook I always carry with me, reading it aloud, voicing it one syllable at a time. *Psoas?* It was a man's name, four Greek letters in the nominative, psi, omicron, alpha, and sigma, *ps-o-a-s*, pronounced SO-az, the *p* silent, and a strange one. But all cultures have names that are common and others that are uncommon.

The curator reappeared. "Ah, you've made yourself at home."

"I hope you don't mind. See, rubber gloves. This is curious, no?" I said, stepping aside to show her the six ostraka I had laid on the table.

"They're all curious," she replied. She donned gloves, gingerly took hold of the largest ostrakon and brought it to a nearby computer. She typed in the accession number with which it was discreetly marked.

"This one and its five mates were unearthed at a sanctuary on Mount Hymettos, near Athens, dedicated to Zeus. Their date has been established with fair precision: *circa* 710 BCE. The writing says, 'I am here because of Psoas of Midea son of nobody.'"

"That's what I made out, too. And you said Mount Hymettos?"

"Yes. Database says we have a second set of ostraka in storage from the same site but from a different hand that says roughly the same thing, finishing at the *s*—of 'son', presumably—and with the word 'here' misspelled. And we have another set, five pieces this time, from a third hand, that also makes reference to Psoas. That one says, 'Psoas fought on until he won his doom.' His *doom*—dark stuff."

"Who was Psoas?" I mused.

"Zeus only knows. Likely these ostraka were the work of students learning how to write, which would explain the wobbly letters and the mistakes. Their teacher was probably a scribe at the sanctuary."

"A peculiar nickname, 'son of nobody'. That would sting in a patriarchal society. Odd to assign to students as practice for their writing a sentence with an insult in it."

"They could be curse tablets—*katadesmoi*."

"But it's early for *katadesmoi*, no? And the wording isn't quite right. If you want a god to hex someone you hate, you want that god's attention. Almost always in a *katadesmos* a god is invoked. Here there's no mention of Zeus, or any other god, only a claim to presence, *I am here*, from a mere mortal. That's strange."

"Strange indeed—welcome to my world. And welcome to Oxford."

I left the Ashmolean. As I returned on foot to Magdalen College,

I reflected on a mild coincidence: I'd been to Mount Hymettos in my backpacking days, after my first stint at university, those rent-free years when I was poor, working at whatever jobs I could find to pay for a bed and some food, teaching English, cleaning dorm rooms and toilets, washing dishes, sometimes sleeping in parks or on beaches, yet wealthy, because I had the world. The ancient sanctuary to Zeus lies just east of Athens, easily reached but rarely visited by tourists, who rather head to Cape Sounion, with its magnificent temple to Poseidon. But I made my way to the sanctuary. It was a place of dark green leaves and tumbledown marble, black-veined with age. I stayed there a number of hours, into the dusk, entirely alone, and that spell of peace cast by the remains of Ancient Greece took hold of me, the work of the softly radiant sun, the gentle wind, the occasional bleating of sheep, and the whispering spirits hiding in the temple ruins. Time slipped by without notice and my mind emptied of worries and troubles, all knots untied, all riddles resolved, replaced by quiet rapture. Everything became clear to me at that moment, but without the desolation of purely cerebral understanding: life is a matter of radiance and simplicity, and the challenge of life is to remain within that radiance and simplicity. I had a small clay jar of honey I'd bought at a roadside stand. In ancient times, Hymettos was famed for its thyme honey. It was as I ate that golden honey with white cheese on a slice of fresh bread in this sanctuary to Zeus that I fell in love with Ancient Greece and decided on a life of classical study. After a few too many years of peaceable drifting and random jobs, Hymettos was my Mount Ararat. I was a late but eager starter.

I wondered now if the strangely named Psoas had also eaten thyme honey on Mount Hymettos. Who was he? What was his story?

In time, I found—more: brought to life—Psoas of Midea. The son of nobody lay buried in ancient papyri and faded codices, even in broken cuneiform tablets, discovered hither and yon, the majority untranslated from their original language, his name often corrupted, as happens with unusual names, but he was there, he was there, with his story to tell.

But on the day I examined those six Ashmolean ostraka, picked up purely by chance, and all in all minor items in the extensive collections of the museum, there was still no *Psoad* (as I came to call the lost epic).

There were only a few ancient student pottery scribblings. So this is not only a story—a Greek epic, to be exact—but the story of a story.

How to tell it, all of it, in the round? At first I thought I might speak about the *The Psoad* in the third person, projecting my voice as from one of those outsize masks of Ancient Greek theatre, my authority loud and clear. That is the standard voice of academia, knowledgeable and slightly impersonal, something like this:

> The Canadian scholar Harlow Donne attempted to hear and tease out from the ancient past the song of a lost Trojan War tradition.

The voices of Athena, goddess of wisdom, and Apollo, god of truth. The third person presents the advantages of balance, perspective, sweep. It's a cooler voice, an exercise of the mind.

But who am I kidding? The Greek mask kept slipping. The technical term for referring to oneself in the third person is *illeism*, and I—your grandfather a high school art teacher, your grandmother an office worker, your father the modest son of a family of average means—am no illeist. The personal narrator is rich in the possibilities of intimacy, proximity, warmth. It lends itself to a crestfallen face and a soft-spoken confession. An example:

> I failed you as a father, Helen, and I failed your mother as a husband.

The voices of Aphrodite, goddess of love, and Ares, god of war.

I will speak in the pages that follow in my own voice, that I-voice that has always loved you, my darling Helen. All along, it's just me. Just me. Your daddy.

These pages are divided in two. There is a top half and there is a bottom half, separated by a black line. It's the common format of a scholarly work: a text and its footnotes. You saw the papers I worked on. I did once aspire to be a proper academic, that's no secret. As I wrote, I imagined reading you a story and pausing from time to time to point something out.

Or perhaps the top of the page is the open window at which your mother and father are exchanging heated words—another kind of epic war—while you are crouched at the bottom of the page, unhappy and upset, trying to hold back your tears.

Whatever the case, you are invited to read in the way your teacher Mrs. Adamson insisted, each line from left to right and each consecutive page from top to bottom. That is the way we children of Homer read.

I have given titles to the fragments of *The Psoad* I managed to excavate, and I have arranged these fragments in the order that seemed to fit most naturally the chronology of Psoas's tale, starting with the *Prologue* and its opening appeal to the divine Muse. This is a traditional feature of Ancient Greek epic. By invoking the gods, bards presented their songs not as cheap clay pots baked in the small kiln of their imagination but as vessels gifted from on-high Olympus—for which reason the people had better listen. The appeal to the Muse created a certain immunity to criticism: *What? You dare find fault with the gods, you earthworm?* It placed a song in a timeless tradition, assuming continuity with the past and, if the bard did a good job, assuring it a future; the lucky bard might even get immortality out of it.

Any quotations from Homer are from the lean and swift-flowing Stephen Mitchell translation.

Footnotes appear at the end of each fragment, with textual quotations as reminders and line numbers to help locate the context, for example, *"Psoas stood in a patch of soil whose wine colour the sun and rain would soon enough wash away"* (114–115). These footnotes are varied, even jumbled, I'll admit, but explanations and recollections are like that, not so tethered to sequence. Time may move in a straight line, but memory does not. These footnotes have their share of things to say. Don't neglect them. We all live lives that are footnotes to a greater story.

It all went wrong, as most wars do. Look where I've ended up. Such horrible, yellowed walls. So little light coming through the windows. Hades could be no worse.

War has always been the locus of appalling possibilities. I had my own indirect encounter with this. When I was a child, I was told repeatedly that I should never ask my grandfather about his war experience. On one occasion, my grandmother was present when my mother delivered this warning, and she nodded sternly in agreement. The subject would upset him, best never to mention it. My older brothers, Luke and David, reinforced the point by dangling spit over my face while holding me pinned to the floor, adding shaking fists, headlocks, and death threats for extra clarity. But at the same time, they did not fail to mention that he had been a real battling soldier in the jungles of Vietnam—artillery fire, land mines, hand-to-hand combat, Agent Orange, blood and guts, that sort of thing. He left the country for which he fought the moment his tour of duty was over, leaving the United States for Canada and never, not once, returning.

My brothers and I called the old man Mr. Wrinkles behind his back, but we could also have called him Mr. Lighthouse, because that would have been nearer to his character. Even though he lived with us for the last years of his life, he was something solitary far offshore that occasionally blinked.

If only the subject had never been mentioned. But I was a child. It was like asking an egg not to hatch. One day when no one else was around, I came up to my grandfather in his comfy chair in the living room as he shook with his Parkinson's and I asked him, "Grandad, what was the war like?" Then I stood, waiting, looking deliberately angelic. Mr. Wrinkles took some time to reply. He was no doubt remembering and selecting, constructing a colourful tale for his grandson. He was not. He turned to me, his lips moving, his mouth making a low gurgle, then a perfectly enunciated whisper came out:

"I fucking hated it."

He was like that: all mumble and slur, then a bolt of clarity. I was shocked at his dropping of the F-bomb. Whatever door I had opened in my grandfather's mind, I quickly closed in mine. I nodded and hurried away. I spent the rest of the day worried that he would mention to the family that I had broached the forbidden topic. At supper that evening, I was quiet, obedient, and omnivorous, polishing off my plate and putting it in the dishwasher. I fled to my bedroom the moment I could. I hoped my grandfather would forget our interaction.

He didn't. It was I who forgot it. Days later, as I was blithely crossing the living room, a claw reached out. Mr. Wrinkles pulled me in, bringing me close to his weathered, poorly shaven face and his bad breath. His voice hoarse, he said, "We are hiding places for monsters," and his whorled blue eyes began to tear up.

I was terrified. He released me and I ran away. That moment sealed our relationship. I essentially avoided my grandfather for the rest of his life, a minute disentanglement of a single root that eventually felled the tree. I admit this with shame. I can come up with excuses. I was seven years old. What was the old man thinking, saying that to a child? But I was a child with a closed heart. What excuse is there for that? I never told my grandfather that he didn't look to me like a hiding place for monsters. I never reached out to touch him, to offer my hand to be held or myself to be hugged. I simply shut the old man out—then bawled my eyes out at his funeral.

He was a man whom war forever distanced from life. I suspect that his Parkinson's, which he had early and for a long time, was the pathological manifestation of an earlier, deeper trembling, when he was a young man at war.

When I came of age, perhaps I was unconsciously drawn to Homer's *Iliad* by my grandfather's comment. He had participated in one of the twentieth century's many Trojan Wars. Why not study the blueprint, the original hiding place for monsters?

So here, Helen, is the result of my own investigations.

ABSTRACT: A Man and His Mistakes. *The Psoad*: A Reconstruction of a Lost Trojan War Tradition.

Donne, H. *Oxford* Ph.D.

A man arrives on a foreign shore. His expedition holds promise and he has high hopes. He strives mightily. It all goes wrong. He has much he could say about that, but his story is lost—until another man arrives on another foreign shore, he too with high hopes.

The most famous stories of the Trojan War and its aftermath are Homer's *Iliad* and *Odyssey*. But these were not the only tales of the war sung to ancient audiences by bards. There were others, now vanished but for echoes and fragments, the whole collected in what has come to be known as the Epic Cycle. In this thesis, I bring to light a lost Trojan War tradition, reclaimed from the past. Whereas in *The Iliad*, Homer's omniscient perspective closely aligns with the point of view of the Greek ruling class, in *The Psoad*, it is commoners who raise their voices, and they have much to say of their experience at Troy.

It is my argument that the heroes of the Epic Cycle, in this case Psoas of Midea, created the space for the appearance of their complement, Jesus of Nazareth, the other foundational figure of Western culture, the other half of the profoundly contradictory Western character, a character able both to hate and to love with unchecked passion.

On the question of what is fact and what is fiction, which will arise naturally, everything to do with early writing, Homer, *The Iliad*, Oxyrhynchus, the Gospels, Midea, and every other observation about the nest in which the Psoadic egg is placed is factually true (as much as facts on these are available), while everything about Psoas and *The Psoad*, the egg itself, is very likely fictional, having no verifiable factual basis. But this is not as useful a distinction as the reader might think, since Homer's *Iliad*—indeed, the whole Trojan War tradition—is also fiction, only better established. We're talking myth here. Both epics are acts of imaginative witness, and in the absence of actual history, they very nicely explain the Ancient Greek world (in fact, they lay its foundations). The bards do something surprising: they make the facts unnecessary. Or, to put it another way, their stories became facts, as solid to build upon.

From hints and scraps, mere hoary whispers from millennia ago, I have managed to construct thirty coherent fragments of *The Psoad*, which I present here in English, with explanatory annotations throughout. The usual disclaimer, then: I am the lone author and sole translator of these Psoadic fragments, and with me lies the blame for all errors, defects, misinterpretations, outrageous distortions, incredible leaps, dubious rounding-offs, flat-out inventions, and any other accusations that might be leveled at an explorer of the remote past foolish enough to attempt to see through faded ink, interrupted sentences, lost connections, and the other ravaging effects of time.

The reconstruction of this Greek epic was a personal affair, which I share in this thesis not because I want to draw attention to myself, but to show that the past is never done with, that always there are parallels and returns and repetitions, always the song continues.

Prologue

Muse, have you forgotten him? Psoas was his name.
Is he to stay in the gloom of Hades,
nevermore to see the honey light of the world?
What did he do to deserve this chill fate?
Let me sing his song—then we'll see where he should stay,
whether in that soaring cave called the mortal mouth,
whence a flutter of the tongue will give him glory,
or in that dank, dark place, silent and bone-chilling,
where unhappy creatures move about like shadows.
Psoas, I say, was his name and he was my friend.   10

"Muse, have you forgotten him?" (1): I can see you at the top of the stairs, a shadow in unicorn pyjamas. You never did like going to sleep. It wasn't that you were afraid of the dark. It was that you thought sleep was a waste of time. Why be unconscious and unaware when you could be awake and having fun? The ritual was always the same.

"Go back to bed, Helen," I would tell you.
"No," you would reply, with fierce conviction.
"It's late. You should be sleeping."
"Don't want to."
"You're tired."
"Am not."
"Do not come down those stairs, young lady."
"Tell me a story."
"I'm working."
"You're always working."
"No I'm not."
"Where's Mommy?"
"She's working. She's having a late night."
"See. You're always working."
"That's not true."

"Tell me a story."
"Go back to bed."
"I'm not going back to bed."
Silence.
"Just one story, *please*," you would plead.
"All right. Come sit here next to me."

You would always win. Does that make me a bad father? But if I set one of those strict boundaries that parenting courses tell you a parent should always set, you would stomp upstairs in a fury and, a minute later, I would hear your far-off voice say, "I'm not sleeping," and then, a minute later, "I'm not sleeping," and then, a minute later, "I'm not sleeping," on and on, like a yipping dog. And if that stopped and there was silence and I tiptoed upstairs, congratulating myself on my parenting excellence, likely as not you would be sitting in bed, eyes wide open, staring down the night, waiting for me. Having successfully lured me into your trap, you would glare at me like a little Gorgon and hiss, "I'm not sleeping"—and then *I* would get into a fury. And if I decided to wait you out, ignoring both your yipping and your silence, then you'd eventually come down again and we'd start all over.

So better just to tell you a story. You would tuck up against me on the sofa, which was always sweet, and sometimes I would pull out a book—I loved reading to you—but more often I would riff on a Greek myth—oh, the torments of Daphne as, fleeing Apollo, she turned first into a mole, then a rock, then an octopus, then an eagle, before settling on a laurel tree—or I would spin a tale out of nothing—do you remember the story of Fresh, the lost tooth who woke up one morning on the banks of the Limpopo River?—until I felt you go limp against me, falling into the arms of Morpheus, as they say, a story doing what a father couldn't.

But on this particular June night that starts our story, in the middle of the usual tense bedtime silence, as we were scowling like fighters about to lunge at each other, you on the stairs, me at my desk, there came from my computer a clear, resonant *ping*. I turned to the screen.

"Oh! Helen, come quick!"

You buffaloed down the stairs. You were there when I first read that email from Oxford. You shared in my joy—we whooped and we hollered, we did the chicken dance, you went to bed far too late—neither of us quite realizing the implication: that I would be leaving you. You only understood that I was really happy.

"Psoas was his name" (1): Never has so much been rescued by so little. *The Psoad*, all of it, would have been missed—lost—were it not for that unusual Ancient Greek name.

"Let me sing his song" (5): I was the delighted, unexpected recipient of a scholarship that plucked me from my academic Pluto on the Canadian Prairies and sent me, comet-like, to the dazzling sun that is Oxford University.

At the news, over breakfast, your mother, Mommy, Gail, my wife, put down her coffee and phone and said, "You're kidding me?"

"Nope," I replied. "I got it. Full academic year, all expenses paid: transportation, room, board, tuition and ancillary fees, everything."

"You said you had no chance of getting it."

"It was a long shot. But extra funding came through, which explains the late notice."

"Well, congratulations, that's great. But now we really have to think about this. What about Helen? Who's going to look after her?"

"I was hoping you could get a leave from work and we could all go to England."

"They're not going to give me a leave for a *year*."

"This is an unbelievable opportunity for me—for us. I'd be working with Franklin Cubitt, one of the world's foremost scholars of the Oxyrhynchus Papyri."

"The what?"

"I'll give you the quick of it. When—"

"I sense a lecture coming."

"Wait. It's actually really interesting. When Alexander the Great died in Babylon in 323 BCE on his way back from his astonishing ten-year march from Macedonia to India, the empire he built was divvied up among his generals. Ptolemy, another Macedonian Greek, got the Egyptian slice of the pie, which he ruled skillfully. HELEN, COME DOWN. BREAKFAST IS READY! The Ptolemaic dynasty lasted three hundred years. It shone with particular brilliance in Alexandria. The Lighthouse of Alexandria, one of the Seven Wonders of the Ancient World, was built by his son, Ptolemy II, and the Great Library of Alexandria was a Greek-language library. It's because of Alexander the Great that the language and culture of the Greeks spread to the whole eastern Mediterranean world, hence Greek-speaking Egyptians and Greek-speaking Jews, people with their feet in two worlds. Hence Greek-written Gospels. Greek culture spread to every—"

"Okay, I hear you're excited, but we have to leave soon."

"Yes, I know. Just another minute—including to a town of some importance south of Cairo named Oxyrhynchus. There was something unusual about Oxyrhynchus. Unlike nearly every other Egyptian town, it didn't lie directly on the Nile but rather along a branch, the Bahr Yussef. That means Oxyrhynchus was never flooded by the waters of the Nile, and it never rains in Oxyrhynchus, never, so when the Bahr Yussef dried up, water left town. Helen, maple syrup or brown sugar on your porridge?"

"Brown sugar. And yoghurt."

"Brown sugar and yoghurt, please. Eat up. The people followed soon after and all life stopped in Oxyrhynchus, including the minute life of organic decay. Garbage in the municipal dump stayed exactly as it was, completely dry and undisturbed. And among the many things the Oxyrhynchites threw out for some seven hundred years, until about 500 CE, were scrolls of papyrus too covered in handwriting to be of any further use. A mountain of—"

"I thought they lived in Australia?"

"You're thinking of the platypus, sweetie. I wonder what a Greek myth about a platypus would be like. We'll have to think about that. Papyrus is a kind of paper made from Egyptian sedge. A mountain of Greek writing, double-sided, lay hidden under the sands of Oxyrhynchus until two British papyrologists, Bernard Grenfell and Arthur Hunt, stumbled upon them in 1896. Drink your milk. It's one of the greatest Egyptian archaeological discoveries, greater than the tomb of Tutankhamun, frankly. Over six busy winters—because the summer heat was unbearable—Grenfell and Hunt excavated. What they found was amazing. It was all there in the city's garbage dump: bills, wills, petitions, official correspondence, court records, lots of personal letters, and literature, too, some of it unknown. Grenfell and Hunt came upon a beautiful poem by Sappho in the stuffing of a mummified crocodile. Even more amazing, they found sayings of Jesus, some unknown, from the Gospel of Thomas. What you get—wait."

I raised my hand. Gail was making to interrupt me again. "I'm nearly done. What you get, finally, with these thousands of glimpses, is a complete picture of an ancient city and its citizens. Volume 1 of *The Oxyrhynchus Papyri* was published in 1898. Volume 87 came out in 2023. At least another thirty volumes are expected. My hope is to be a contributing author."

"Okay, Professor Donne, I get it. But where's *Mutilations of the Corpse in* The Iliad? Where's Homer and your thesis in all this? What did Gordon say?"

"Well, as a matter of fact, you find a lot of Homer on Greek papyri. He was by far the most popular writer of the time. The original bestseller. As for Gordon the Gordian Knot, in a small department in a small university, every mule has to pull more than one cart. My weary thesis supervisor said what he always says, 'Just find something to say.' I don't think he really cares what I do for the year. He—"

Gail's phone pinged.

"That text can wait, no? I guess not. Come on, Helen, eat up or you'll be late for school. Anyway, it's not my Homeric scholarship they want me for so much as my knowledge of Ancient Greek. It's pretty good. And it's Oxford. It has the largest Faculty of Classics in the world."

"Sorry?"

"You want me to turn down a scholarship to Oxford?"

"You want me to quit my job?"

She was always the practical one, Gail was. But is life a practical affair? She didn't like her job, was always complaining about it. The hours, the pressure, the stress.

"And what if you did? You want to be doing something you love. And think of it: a year in England."

"Someone has to earn a living in this family, Harlow. Homer pays minimum wage."

In the balance of life, what is the weight of a dream, what is the weight of reality? Which tips the scale?

"Okay, we gotta go," continued Gail. "You're going shopping today, right? Vanilla extract, don't forget. And the cottage cheese with no added salt."

"Let's talk about it later, Gail. Think of what it will do for my career. You and Helen could come visit me for Christmas, at the very least. Go, go, go, girl, get your shoes on and out the door! Wait, bowl in the dishwasher. Helen, did you know that Alexander the Great slept with a copy of Homer's *Iliad* under his pillow?"

"Under his *pillow*?"

"Yeah."

"He must have had a sore neck every morning."

Out we hurried, all three of us, Gail to her job as an executive at a meat-packing company, I had tutoring that morning, and you had school.

But two fighters would circle back to scowl at each other.

"where unhappy creatures move about like shadows" (9): "This morning, you really couldn't listen for five minutes? And I didn't appreciate that line about Homer paying minimum wage, and you said it right in front of Helen. What does that say to her about the value of a life of the mind?"

"She's seven, Harlow."

"It's the tone, the *tone*. She's not deaf to that. And I've been looking after her ever since you went back to work, while studying and tutoring pretty much full time. That's a lot of work for little pay, you're right, but both the little girl *and* Homer are investments that will pay off."

"*Looking after her?* What, you're a single dad? She doesn't have a mother?"

"You work long hours."

"I do, and then I come home and I also look after our daughter."

"I missed that part, many evenings and weekends."

"Of course you have. You're very good at rewriting history."

"No, I'm good at reading it. And you know what, getting back to the topic of Oxford, I think the time apart might do us good. A bit of breathing space. A chance to reset."

Gail stared hard at me. "Really? The good dad thinks sailing off to Troy will solve our problems? How did that work out for the Greeks?"

"As I just said, it's the tone, the *tone*."

And so it started, as it always did, with the appearance of a single pinpoint of resentment that called forth another pinpoint, then another and another, tit for tat, until, out of nothing, in the evening quiet of a bedroom, shimmered the complete outline of a domestic dispute, a bright constellation of infinite acrimony. All that was needed now was to fill in the contours with colour, which we did wholeheartedly. We tensed our bodies, set our faces, fixed our eyes, hardened our tones. Our every accusation called forth another, valid or tenuous, shouted or hissed, no matter, so long as it hit the mark. We urged each other on, harder and deeper, loading our words with as much malice as they could carry, digging into each other's weaknesses, mocking each other's strengths, adding new twists, more fire, further venom, revived outrage, what you want, to the old story, reminding ourselves that no grievance was forgiven and none was forgotten. It went on and on, until exhaustion ground us to a halt and we lay in bed, our backs to each other, the silence glaring, the emotional temperature glacial.

Is there anything more tedious or more draining than the arguments of a relationship on the rocks? That's the one part of *The Iliad* I've never liked, toward the end of Book 3. Bring me arrogance and folly, bring me fire and destruction, bring me doom and the collapse of entire civilizations—just don't bring me household squabbles. Helen is summoned by Aphrodite, disguised as a beloved old servant, to go to Paris, who is in their bedchamber. The summons is gentle, an enticement, but when Helen resists, Aphrodite shows her divine form, in full fury, and the quaking mortal naturally submits. In their sumptuous nest, Helen is as mercurial as Aphrodite: at first she berates Paris for his ineptness on the battlefield, then they make love. Helen has good reason to be upset. Paris has just fought a duel with Menelaus that was supposed to settle, one way or the other, the disastrous, years-long conflict between the Greeks and the Trojans, the individual victor winning the whole war for his side, but Aphrodite shrouding Paris in a dense mist and whisking him away before Menelaus could kill him stalled the duel, and then a Trojan archer, Pandarus, tricked by Athena into shooting Menelaus and wounding him, has cancelled it. The duel is over, the war is back on.

That is how Greek epic works, on a grand scale, with outsize characters and enthralling scenes, and it's a dandy. But Helen's harsh words, Paris's deflections, a couple bickering, then the placebo of sex—Homer, can you please leave that out of Greek epic? Domestic quarrels, because so petty and personal, so undignified, don't fit well in public song.

You were in the next room, in your bed. Were you still asleep, Helen? I doubt it. I'm sorry for all the arguments you heard. It didn't do any of us any good. In Greek epic, no one listens and no one gets along. Then there's hell to pay.

The Layout of the Ships

Between the mighty ships of the two great kings,
Zeus-like Agamemnon's one hundred sea-borne
fortresses, and those of his brother, fierce
Lord Menelaus's sixty grand warships,
rested on the sands the awe-striking vessels
of god-feared Lord Diomédes, eighty in all.
And next to these, on the Agamemnon side,
lying in wait like a lion about to pounce,
crouched the forty proud ships of Midea,
on which arrived Psoas, the son of nobody.   10
"What a magnificent sight, our armada of
one thousand one hundred and eighty-six warships!"
said he. "We will make good of our time here.
To take from the rich Trojans, what a dream."

The Layout of the Ships **(title)**: Before ships can rest on sand they must first arrive on a shore, so this fragment in Psoas's tale is chronologically in the wrong place. It should come fourth, after the *Prologue* and the two *Arrival* fragments (to come), but I place it here, at the beginning, because it was the fragment that got me started, the first fragment of *The Psoad* I discovered, assembled from eighty-one shreds of papyrus.

"the two great kings" (1): Agamemnon of Mycenae and his brother, Menelaus of Sparta, are the dominant kings of the Greek expedition to Troy. And the coveted object of the war they are about to fight for ten long years is Agamemnon's famed sister-in-law, Menelaus's transcendentally beautiful and feisty wife, Helen, now the consort of Prince Paris, son of King Priam of Troy, your namesake, my well-named daughter.

"god-feared Lord Dioméd*es*" (6): Isn't god-*fearing* the usual sentiment of mortals toward gods? But the bard is correct. One of the mightiest heroes of the Trojan War, Dioméd*es* is judged by Homer to be second only to Achilles and Ajax in prowess, and he is feared with good reason even by his gods. In *The Iliad*, he injures both Aphrodite and Ares in battle, the first by stabbing her in the wrist with his spear, causing her terrible pain. She shrieks and withdraws from the field, whimpering. The pain he inflicts on Ares is even worse. It is, quite literally, visceral:

> Then Diomédes thrust with his spear, and Athena
> guided it, and it plunged into Ares' belly
> at the place where his bronze kilt was fastened, and after it tore
> into his flesh, she pulled the spear out again.
> And Ares bellowed; his roar was as loud as the shout
> of ten thousand men as they join in the tumult of battle. (5.855–861)

A god who suffers in body and spirit like Jesus descends from the Greeks.

"lying in wait like a lion about to pounce" (8): "So you're sure about this, Gail? You'll be all right?"

Once we'd calmed down, we talked about it again. Finally, you're the one who made it possible. You brightly opined that I should go. That was you: always game, always willing.

"Helen and I will manage just fine. You deserve it. It'll be good for you and your career."

"It'll be good for *us*."

"Right. And for Homer."

"Him, too. Okay, then I'll say yes to Oxford. Thank you."

All the arrangements were made: forms were signed, flights were booked, and suitcases were packed. The day of departure came. At the airport, I was happy, because I was excited by the adventure I was embarking on, and I was sad, because I was leaving you behind. You were sad, perhaps you regretted giving me permission to leave but you weren't going to go back on your word, and you were happy, for me. As for your mother, well, in Homer you never hear words like Agamemnon *thought*, or Nestor *remembered*, or Odysseus *reflected*, and so on. In Ancient Greek epic, characters express themselves strictly through action or through speech. It's not as if the Ancient Greeks didn't think, remember, or reflect, but in their epics they chose not to reveal this interior life, the turning of their mental cogs, an early example of the creative writing injunction *Show, don't tell*. When we were saying goodbye, Gail's expression was neutral and fixed. Perhaps she was sad. Or anxious about her stint as a single parent. Or worried about work, maybe that too. However it was she felt, when I came to kiss her, she turned her face and offered me a cheek. Being an action, it was properly Homeric.

Then she spoke close up to me, her warm breath pulsing against my ear. "Don't come back," she whispered.

"lying in wait like a lion about to pounce" (8): I knocked on an ancient wooden door and entered an ornate office, Oxford at its most Gothic, with stone walls and pointy windows, in addition to crammed bookshelves and a leather chair and sofa.

Before me, sitting at a solid wooden desk, was a man of surprisingly great age, older-looking than in any photo I had seen online, bald except for wisps of white hair on the sides of his head, like clouds on a horizon, and piercing eyeballs that fixed me like an eagle set to land its talons on a prey. He was dressed in a suit, the colours pale except for the deep blue tie. His clothes clashed with his face and hands, the freshness of the fabric contrasting sharply with the wear of his features. I found out later that Franklin Cubitt was eighty-three years old and this had been his office for over fifty years.

"Good morning. Professor Cubitt?"

"I beg your pardon?"

"Are you Professor Cubitt?"

"A bit louder. Yes, I am. And you are the new young man from America. Sit down."

Oh, the bejewelled accent, the haughty mien. My plain accent and I, commoners both, sat on the sofa he had pointed to.

"From Canada, actually."

"Is that so? My mistake. Your name?"

"Harlow Donne."

"Let me find your file. Here it is. Right. Yes, I remember. Not from Princeton, Harvard, or Yale, but from the University of the Unpronounceable. A ridiculous name, in passing. An institution should have no more than two syllables to its appellation, three tops."

"I will tell the chancellor that."

He took the comfy chair opposite me.

"Have you settled in?"

"Well, I got here yesterday. Lovely train ride from London. Everything so green. I guess it's all that rain."

"Such a tiresome cliché. Where are you staying?"

"At Holywell Ford."

"Of course. What do you think of the college so far?"

"Magdalen is absolutely stunning, rain or sunshine."

"It's pronounced Maudlin—Maudlin College. If you're going to spend time here, you might as well say it correctly. Welcome to the Faculty of Classics. All right, enough chit-chat. My expectations, Mr.—what was your name again?"

"Harlow Donne."

"My expectations, Mr. Harlow, are faultless punctuality, unremitting attention to detail, and ceaseless industry. The Oxyrhynchus Papyri are a great monument and you are a worker ant whose selfless efforts should be exemplary. You are here to move bits of leaves, one after the other, into the light of *significance*. It is a beautiful task. Now, let's have a cup of tea and see if you have what it takes. Tell me about the optative mood in Ancient Greek. Milk? Sugar?"

He served me tea so strong it would dissolve coins, and for the next hour he grilled me on the minutiae of Ancient Greek grammar. He had at hand a selection of Oxyrhynchus Papyri, reproductions, of course, from the Ptolemaic, Roman, and Byzantine periods, and he led me down winding paths, asking me to explain, where I might, the varying uses of the optative mood, in temporal expressions, for example, or, in one selection, in expressions of fear, a task made treacherous by the fact that some of the ancient writers were careless or ill-educated. I was to guard from making mistakes while catching the mistakes of others, on ragged shreds, the writing faint.

I left his office exhausted. But I seemed to have passed muster. The last thing he said to me was, "You will start tomorrow."

He had asked me hardly any personal questions. He was all business. A man and his archaeology.

"*Psoas, the son of nobody*" (10): [*ring*]
[*ring*]
"Hello, sweetie."
[*meeting ended*]
[*ring*]
"Helen, it's Daddy."
[*meeting ended*]
[*ring*]
"Don't hang up!"
[*meeting ended*]
[*ring*]
"Helen, pass the phone to Mommy!"
[*meeting ended*]
[*ring*]
[*ring*]
[*ring*]
[*ring*]

You refused to talk to me. You too were all business. A daughter and her dismay. You had realized that I would not be there for your birthday. But I had not forgotten you. Oxford's Museum of Natural History holds the world's last surviving remains of the dodo, that plump, flightless, ridiculous-looking bird from Mauritius, eternally famous for being extinct. I had got you a dodo bird kit for your birthday. There was a book and a game, there was a model you could make with plaster of Paris—it was really well done. And I had managed to find a stuffy of a platypus. I had mailed all this in good time, including a card and a small framed photo of me standing in front of the herd of deer that live on the grounds of Magdalen College.

I missed you. I had no one to tell stories to at bedtime now. Did you feel the silence too?

"Psoas, the son of nobody" (10): *Don't come back.* How could Gail say that to me? I was in shock. When you fight, at least you're still there. You're still there.

"Psoas, the son of nobody" (10): Psoas? *Psoas?* Is there a Greek god of surprises? Here I was in Oxyrhynchus—or, rather, on the second floor of the Bodleian Ancient World Library, as it was now called, in the Papyrology Work Room, barely two weeks into my work, sitting at my desk—when Psoas appeared before my eyes, rising from shreds of papyrus like Ozymandias from the lone and level sands of the Sahara.

Ancient papyrus comes in shades of pale brown against which the faded black of ancient ink stands out nicely. It's rougher than paper; the fibre of the plant from which it was made can be seen with the plain eye. It tends to tear or fall apart along the grain of the fibre, which, depending on the direction of the writing on it, is either helpful—you get a vertical column of truncated words whose meaning can possibly be construed when placed next to another column—or unhelpful: you get a few words that just float.

That morning, three or four dozen papyrus fragments, carefully removed from a folder, were resting before me on a sheet of acid-free paper. The finds at Oxyrhynchus, for all their remarkable preservation, are in tatters. I had delicately brushed away any dirt, I had the microscope hovering in the air to my left, to my right I had the tiny trowel and various tweezers with which to move the fragments, and I had paper and pen—I was set. This was my joyful daily work now: to shuffle bits of darkness until light broke through.

The pieces shifted under my hovering fingers. Here? Like this? Maybe this way? Along here? Some scraps came together, like Brazil embracing Africa, the plate tectonics suddenly obvious, and along the tears I faintly made out a phrase, in Ancient Greek, of course: "—rived Psoas, the son of no—". I looked more carefully through the microscope. It took me some seconds to compute what I had stumbled upon. When I saw the name—realized it—a quavering "MAH!" came out of me. One or two fellow graduate students nearby raised their heads and looked over at me.

I pulled out my notebook and found the page. There it was, from the Ashmolean ostraka, *I am here because of Psoas of Midea son of nobody*. The same name, the same insult. I gasped, marvelled—then dismissed. The ages and places of origin were so divergent. The Ashmolean ostraka, unearthed near Athens, dated to roughly 700 before Christ, while this batch of Oxyrhynchus Papyri, uncovered in the sands of Egypt, came from the third century *after* Christ. A distance of some nine hundred years and over a thousand kilometres, with an ocean in between. Psoas might very well have been an ordinary name at the time. Names cross history with little fanfare, appearing, enduring, disappearing, reviving. It was a name, only that. Despite the identical insult—it too perhaps common—they must be different Psoases.

I returned to the scraps again, hoping to expand an island into a small landmass. Mercifully, the Oxyrhynchite who had disposed of this leaf of papyrus had not scattered it into the wind. In less than an hour, I managed to collate another snippet. Psoas had arrived on "the forty proud ships of Midea" (9). Same name, same insult, and now same city. A triple coincidence didn't seem credible. It had to be the same man.

By noon, three kings appeared in eight preceding lines, rough and ragged, but still legible. I marvelled again. The bard clearly meant to place the men of Midea in exalted company, at the heroic heart of the Greek forces, so:

Agamemnon	Midea	Diomédes	Menelaus
100 ships	40 ships	80 ships	60 ships

But what, Midea had no king worth naming? Instead, three great Iliadic heroes were placed next to a low-born? The juxtaposition couldn't be more clashing, the deliberate opposition stated more starkly.

"What a magnificent sight, our armada of one thousand one hundred and eighty-six warships!" (11–12): By three o'clock, I came across four more lines. At the sight of the size of the fleet, my heart jumped. According to Homer in his Catalogue of Ships in Book 2 of *The Iliad*, 1,186 is the number of ships in the Greek armada that sailed to Troy. Like some historical numbers—1066, 1215, 1492, 1789, 1914, for example, to people of the West—1,186 is a famous number in the world of classical scholarship, instantly and highly associative. It is a number that is bolted to the story of the Trojan War.

For a papyrus newbie, this was a heady day of swashbuckling scholarship. I was ecstatic.

Just then, rolling in like a thundercloud, his cane ominously tapping on the floor, Professor Cubitt arrived to do his daily inspection of his minions' work.

"Professor Cubitt, look what I've found. The Trojan War!"

He glanced at my finds and merely grumbled. "Gah! More bloody *Iliad*! File it away, Mr. Harlow. We already know the authors the Oxyrhynchites liked to read, same as everyone everywhere. Homer in Oxyrhynchus is no different from Homer in Corinth."

You'd think I'd be crestfallen, but I wasn't. I was not so hardened as Franklin Cubitt. To find a whiff of the Trojan War, scented by the passage of well over a millennium and a half, perhaps dictated, the speaking mouth singing to the writing hand, a living bard passing on the Bard to an original amanuensis—it took my breath away.

Cubitt was wrong. He was an economic historian by training, not a classicist. This wasn't the work of the Bard. In *The Iliad*, there are over seven hundred named characters, from the immortal gods and the immortally known heroes and women, both Greek and Trojan, to the lesser characters, to the extras who are named just before they are killed off. Each is accounted for, however briefly, by Homer; it is a kindness on his part to give everyone an obituary before they are expedited to Hades, so that they might not be entirely forgotten. I wasn't positively sure at that moment, but I had a good hunch that there was no Greek fighter by the name of Psoas in *The Iliad*. If it had been Achilles, son of Peleus, or Odysseus, son of Laertes, in a scene I recognized, then the connection would have been clear and definitive, and I would have happily laid stake to this conventional bit of Homerica and proudly consigned it to Volume 88 of *The Oxyrhynchus Papyri*. Instead, it was an unknown son of nobody. And there was something even more problematic.

"But, sir, look, look." I pointed at where Psoas's forty proud ships had come from. "It says the ships came from Midea."

"So?"

"Midea is never mentioned in *The Iliad*."

On that point, I was certain.

Professor Cubitt sighed. "Congratulations, Mr. Harlow, you've discovered some pseudo-Homerica. Every age produces its plagiarizers, fabricators, pasticheurs, con men, and liars. What you've got there is the derivative dross of a wannabe. No doubt he was trying to impress a girl. Now what's on the verso of those fragments, that's what I'd like to know? A money account, perhaps? A letter from a legal supplicant? *That* would be of greater interest."

"Thank you for the clarification, sir."

I closed shop and ventured out of the Ancient World Library into the raw English evening, those jaws of damp that, already in October, were gnawing at my bones.

A surge of energy—physical, intellectual, creative—coursed through me. I decided to walk it off. During the day, the streets of Oxford are overwhelmed by hordes of tourists, rivers of them, their wheeled suitcases loudly rumbling on the cobblestones. But now, as the day darkened, the streets began to empty, and all the stone of Oxford, lacquered with rain, shone untroubled under the streetlights. Without your hand in my hand, without your voice in my ears, I walked and walked and walked, my face blank while my mind, strapped to the mast of a ship, was in the thrall of a Siren's song.

Midea's absence in Homer is strange. The town counted as one of the great Mycenaean fortified citadels, with a view that is breathtaking. It sat atop a rocky hill, one side protected by sheer cliffs, the other girded by the same "Cyclopean walls" as Mycenae and Tiryns, with stones of such monumental bulk that later Greeks thought only giant Cyclops could have set them in place. Midea dominated the eastern edge of the Argolid plain. To the southwest of it lay Tiryns, praised by Homer as "mighty-walled", and the residence of Hercules during his Twelve Labours—speaking of which, Hercules' father was Zeus but his mother, Alcmene, was from Midea, born and bred, among Midea's own fair share of mythological connections. Its fortifications were said to have been devised by Perseus, he who slew Medusa and saved Andromeda from the sea monster (and another son of Zeus). Directly across from Midea was Argos, the seat of fearsome King Diomédes. And lastly, most impressive of all, close by to the northwest, in Mycenae, reigned King Agamemnon, the formidable supreme commander of the Greek armies at Troy. That's a neighbourhood of some mythological heft.

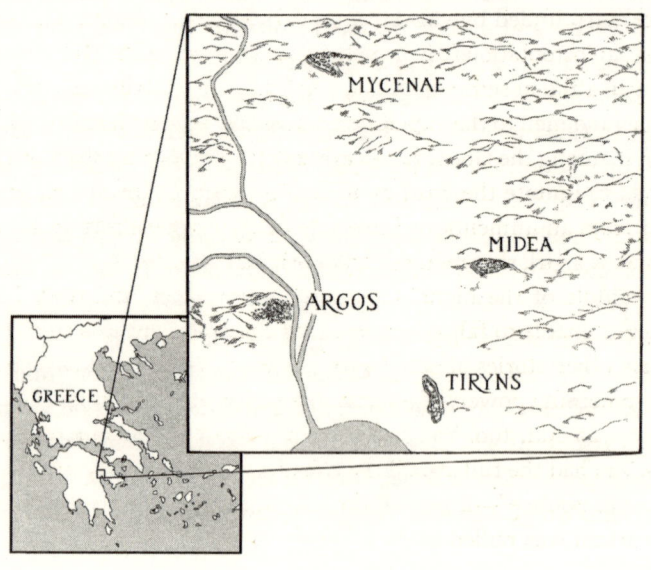

And in real terms, when Midea's royal cemetery at Dendra, about three kilometres away, was excavated, it revealed some of the richest funereal finds of the Mycenaean period, including three pairs of horses ritually sacrificed upon the death of their owners. The horses are laid out on their sides in a graceful manner, surrounded by various precious objects, as attentively buried as humans. It's an ostentatious display of their owners' wealth. Midea was without a doubt an affluent settlement, and it would have contributed a good number of heroes and men to the expedition across the Aegean Sea. For Homer not to mention it among the Greek forces against Troy is nothing short of glaring.

How odd to imitate the Bard by invoking—with an insult—an unknown commoner from an unmentioned town. For a derivative effort by a wannabe seeking to wow a girl, that seemed rather original.

In the middle of the night, I returned to my room and settled in bed, exhausted but unable to fall asleep. Perhaps this fragment was from the Epic Cycle, those other stories about the Trojan War, not as good as Homer, but there was something powerful about it, the poetic scansion. It resonated. And the content was odd, too. You had the big names, Agamemnon, Menelaus, Diomédes, you had the full armada, you had a vivid simile, "lying in wait like a lion about to pounce"—it had all the classic elements of an epic drum roll, then the curtain was pulled back, and who was revealed in the spotlight on centre stage? A nobody, or, to be exact, the son of a nobody, which did nothing to improve his prospects.

"what a dream" (14): The words of my PhD supervisor in Canada, Professor Gordon MacPherson, came to my mind: "Just find something to say." I scanned the lines in my head, the Ancient Greek singing:

> And next to these, on the Agamemnon side,
> lying in wait like a lion about to pounce,
> crouched the forty proud ships of Midea,
> on which arrived Psoas, the son of nobody. (7–10)

I wondered: might this be the beginning of something to say?

The Arrival: The Porcupine's Back

The merchants on board who knew these parts best
looked bewildered. They cast their eyes about,
consulted among themselves in whispers,
but they were certain. "This is it. We have arrived."

"These scrubby hills, that common beach? Are you sure?"
Agamemnon asked, his eyes on the coast.

"Yes, this is the city of Priam. This is Troy."

Our oars dipped once, twice, thrice, our ships surged once,
    twice, thrice,
we groaned with glad strain as we flew across the sea,
our sails puffed out like a proud Argive's chest—   10

what a magnificent sight, our armada of
one thousand one hundred and eighty-six warships—
before the merchants added, "The harbour has changed.
But still you will make good of your time here.
To take from the rich Trojans, what a dream."

"*What* harbour?" asked the great king. "I see none."

Replied Thromachis of Kos, a merchant,
"Precisely. The harbour seems to have vanished.
But the waters are deep. We are safe, my lord.
I have been here often, I know of what I speak."   20
(Very soon, for his words, Thromachis would be dead,
thrown into those deep waters by the king himself,
leaving behind a wife, three sons and a daughter
who would all miss him greatly, him and his stories.)

Wordy Thromachis went on at his peril,

teaching a man who did not want to be taught—
did he not see his stare? "Troy has two harbours.
Just north is a headland—see there, Cape Sigeum?—
whose twin is Cape Rhoeteum. The brothers
face the narrow strait of the Hellespont   30
and between them ships from that vital channel
can slip with ease, pushed by the winds and currents,
into a bay, Trojan Bay it is called.
Those are the haven waters closest to Troy,
with a handy harbour at the city's feet.
We merchants berth there, pay tolls, haggle and bargain,
say yes or no, shake hands, give and take, tally.
We make the Trojans rich, as we make ourselves rich.
Business done, heavy again with new goods,
we row our laden ships to the mouth of the bay,   40
where we turn westward and gallop like horses
through the waves into our native pasture,
the blue Aegean Sea, embraced by Poseidon

and held on course by Boreas. Alas,
the approach to this harbour from the Aegean
is more taxing. Your sails will sag, your rowers tire.
So the clever Trojans, ever eager to trade,
built a second harbour on their western shore—
look, straight ahead. No need to round any cape now,
no need to fight Poseidon or Boreas.   50
They hired Cyclops to clear the water of rocks,
Aegyptians to build the sturdy stone piers,
and Lydians to build the timber jetties.
The gods themselves, Apollo and Hephaestus,
wove all the moorings, those thin strong ropes of fame.
The jetties reached far out to sea, like fingers,
greeting our ships and plucking them free of cargo.
Off we went now around the cape, light as cork,
child's play, to dock below Troy and resupply,
then either to return home or, if further trade   60
was wanted up the Hellespont, to wait,

sometimes for weeks, for the tricky winds to turn,
paying the Trojans, of course, for their hospi—"

"WHAT HARBOUR?" roared the king, cutting the
   merchant short.

Listen to me, to my soul-wrecking tale,
and hear why wordy Thromachis lost his life.
When they heard of our fleet heading their way,
the Trojans dismantled their western harbour,
timber by timber, stone block by stone block,
every jetty and pier, the soaring lighthouse.   70
They tied sharp stakes to the pier blocks and set them
in the moorage waters, row upon row,
so that on arriving in the Troad, instead
of gliding into the finest harbour
of the Aegean, a wonder of the world,
we fell upon a porcupine's hackled back.

Timber cracked like thunder, ships groaned and lurched,
men were swallowed by waves as if by starving eels.

Ten ships from Laconia we lost right away,
brought by Helen-robbed, red-faced Menelaus,   80
then many more, from all over Achaea.
By the time we realized what was happening,
it was too late: our thousand ships were pressing in,
as the winds were good and we were eager.

It was Psoas, the son of nobody,
who said it first. I was there, I heard him.
Lakander, a potter from Dendra, heard him, too,
and hollered it: "RUN A SHIP ALONG THE SHORELINE!"
Another, on a near ship, understood at once.
Odysseus, King of Ithaca, it was,   90
clever then, clever now, clever always.
He said it even louder and gave orders,

making the idea his own, but theft
is a king's right. (Talk to Epéüs about that.)

Promptly it was done: driven by oars, a hull,
striking the stakes from the side, broke many
before it was pierced and took in water.
Twenty ships we lost in this way, in no time,
before our eyes, while we sat, as if at a play,
many men in each—had the war even started? 100
But zigzagging to and fro, these ships cut a swath
in the waters broad enough to save our fleet,
though not before thirty more collided and sank,
fast friends becoming forced foes. Such wreckage!

Later, from shore, we sent skiffs with men tied to ropes
who jumped into the water with knives to cut loose
the remaining stakes. It was perilous work.
We lost more brave men, drowned deep or from tipped skiffs.

So it was that before we even reached land,
already men were dead, widows were made, 110
children were fatherless and hearts were sundered—
because what is a man to do in water?
Our ships never lulled our fear of water.
When a storm hit and a vessel pitched and rolled
and water as solid as a bull jumped aboard
and thundered down the decks, we rowed in terror,
the blades of our oars slashing at the mad sea.
Before water, the bravest man cowers.
(We saw that later with no less than Achilles,
when he faced the fury of Lord Scamander, 120
as the river god strove mightily to catch him
with his long liquid arms and bandy sandy legs.
How the son of Peleus struggled! How he cried!
He whimpered like a child, the only time
we saw that hero humbled, quaking with fear.)

Upon the shore the Trojans awaited us,
clanging their spears against their shields and jeering,
cheered by the success of their brazen scheme.
Among them, standing proud and fierce, was Prince Mestor,
one of the fifty sons of King Priam,   130
one of the fifty suns of sacred Troy.

We reached shallow sands and started to die
as hails of spears and arrows landed on us.
With our feet we had to fight waves of water,
while with our hands we had to fight waves of men.

There is much here to unpack:

"like a proud Argive's chest" (10): In *The Iliad*, Homer calls the Greek-speaking enemies of the Trojans by various names: Argives, Achaeans, or Danäans. In the fragments of his epic found so far, the Psoadic bard uses the first term over fifty times, the second only once, and the third not at all. This is likely an indication that *The Psoad* was born and flourished first in the Kingdom of Argolis, of which Argive is the adjective, which would make sense since that is where Midea, the birthplace of Psoas, is located. In modern times, these same people have collectively been called Mycenaeans. The Mycenaeans lived divided up into twenty or so small, squabbling kingdoms. It would be many centuries before these notably bellicose peoples bonded as one and called themselves Greek.

"what a dream" (15): For a few weeks after stumbling upon Psoas of Midea for the second time, I busied myself trying to see into the social and economic lives of the Oxyrhynchites, but the son of nobody lay on the edge of my consciousness, quietly calling out to me. Then I woke up late one morning, late for a meeting with Professor Cubitt, and I knew I had to heed that call. I had to follow the trail of the name and the town. If there was more to Psoas of Midea, he would surely show up again somewhere.

I turned to the infinite Bodleian Library, figuring that the sands of Oxyrhynchus had given all they could, and there one afternoon, after much labour and some luck (and a lot of complaining from Professor Cubitt about my feckless unreliability, see the scars on my back), I came upon a microfilm of a mimeograph of a fourth-century CE text in the collection of a Venetian library. The pages belonged to a genre called a chrestomathy, which is a compilation of passages from various authors to help in the learning of a language, in this case, a Latin aid to learning Greek. I was skipping over the expository Latin, jumping from Homer to Homer to more Homer, all of it in Greek and familiar, with the regular appearance of Hesiod, Plato, Aristotle, Thucydides, and other authors.

My eyes were glazing over. This reel had a lot of odds and ends on it; it was a waste of my time. I began spinning the little wheel that controlled the microfilm faster and faster—when my eyes were arrested by three Latin words: *clancularius pseudo-Homerica*. Already *pseudo-Homerica* held promise, but even more arresting was *clancularius*, which can be translated as "anonymous" but more usually was used to mean "concealed". I turned the wheel to the selection of twenty-four lines of verse and read it carefully. Agamemnon ... the city of Priam ... oars dipping, sails puffed out—then my eyes fell upon the middle lines:

> what a magnificent sight, our armada of

one thousand one hundred and eighty-six warships—
before the merchants added, "The harbour has changed.
But still you will make good of your time here.
To take from the rich Trojans, what a dream. (11–15)

I leaned back in my chair and took a deep breath. Language tends to fail in times of surprise and fall back on cliché: the discovery felt like a bolt—Zeus-thundered—from the Aegean blue sky. The reference to the armada used the same words, the exact same line repeated, as I had found earlier in the Oxyrhynchus fragment *The Layout of the Ships*. And then there was the repetition of the covetous reassurance, with only a change of person. In the first instance, it was Psoas expressing pleasure at his future good fortune; here, it is the merchants reassuring Agamemnon. I had found two references to a Psoas of Midea and now two references to a magnificent armada of one thousand one hundred and eighty-six ships and the anticipated rewards of that armada's arrival at Troy—and there was an overlap, these references were connected. Surely there would be more to the story.

I generated a copy of the relevant page of the chrestomathy and ran out of the Bod, in a jubilant state. I read the twenty-four lines over and over. Puzzled merchants, an incredulous Agamemnon, a vanished harbour, a doomed merchant from Kos named Thromachis. What was all this about?

The next day I returned and read through the Venetian chrestomathy once more. There was nothing in it of further interest. Then I searched the Bodleian from top to bottom for vanished Trojan harbours and merchants from Kos that might qualify as concealed pseudo-Homerica. It was a fruitless effort. I decided to return to Oxyrhynchus, which, in retrospect, was the obvious step to take. If a fragment of *The Psoad* was found on one leaf of a roll of shredded papyrus, was it not likely that more fragments would be found on that same roll or another? And indeed, after extensive digging, that was where I found the rest of wordy Thromachis's speech and the aftermath of his reassurances to Agamemnon, a hundred and twenty lines brought together from hundreds of papyrus wisps.

"what a dream" (15): Years earlier, back home, at that University of the Unpronounceable, at a term-start meeting of master's students, someone took the empty seat next to me. At the sight of her, I felt genuine astonishment; it was as if a wind blew through me. My pulse quickened.

"Hi," I said quietly.

She turned. "Oh. Hi."

Despite my amazement, which normally would have trussed up my tongue like a chicken about to be roasted, or a body about to be buried at sea, or a hostage being transferred from one hideaway to another, I managed to speak.

"What's your area of study?" I asked.

"Business. And you?" she replied.

A voice like polished marble, smooth and firm. A gaze that was unhesitating; she looked and took me in. And a question, she had asked me a question. How easily she could have answered, then hustled me off by turning her head back to the front of the room, as perfunctory as a passport officer. But instead she had asked a question. A dialogue was on!

"Classics. Homer."

"My minor for my undergraduate degree was English."

"So, why are you studying business now?"

"It's interesting—and practical. Why are you studying Homer?"

"It's interesting—and impractical. How is business interesting to you? I've always found the transactional nature of commerce dispiriting. You buy so that you don't have to relate. You buy distance."

"Still, commerce is a part of life, essential and unavoidable. Homer was a successful businessman. He sold his shaggy-dog stories to lots of buyers. And what if it's not distance that you're buying but freedom and peace? I mean, how many people do you actually want to relate to? Every time you order a hamburger or a coffee, you really want to start chanting *Om shanti* with the waiter or the barista? I'd find that exhausting."

I laughed. She had a quick mind, a nimble sense of humour. And so well dressed! Atop a mustard yellow, knee-length corduroy skirt, she wore a brown vest decorated with embroidered flowers out of which billowed the sleeves of a light, white blouse. The buttons of the vest were each a different bright colour: blue, red, green, yellow. It was a quirky, stylish outfit. The girl had flair. I glanced at her skirt. I love corduroy, how its soft ribs look like a ploughed field, and what a joy to walk around feeling like the fertile earth. When I was a boy, I had a succession of treasured corduroy pants that I wore until the knees and seat of each went completely bald. I had the urge to reach over and touch her on the knee, as if to assess the fabric. In fact, I realized, disbelief was swirling in my mind and I wanted to verify of this person, *Are you real?*

"Nice fedora," she said, complimenting the hat resting on my lap, my one accessory.

I asked her name and we talked for a few precious minutes in whispers before we were called to attention by the emirs of academia at the front of the room. I remember nothing of what they said. When the meeting ended, my neighbour the business student rose from her seat.

I jumped up, and dared. "Do you want to get a bite to eat?"

And that is how I met your mother.

"leaving behind a wife, three sons and a daughter who would all miss him greatly, him and his stories" (23–24): I was reminded of one of my favourite letters from Oxyrhynchus. A schoolboy is writing to his father, whom he misses. This is what this Ancient Greek boy says:

> A nice thing to do, not taking me with you to the city. If you refuse to take me with you to Alexandria, I will not write you a letter or speak to you or wish you good health. If you refuse to take me, this is what happens. A nice thing to do, sending me these grand presents, a hill of beans. Well then, send for me, I beg you. If you don't send for me, I won't eat, I won't drink. There! I pray for your health. Deliver to Theon from Theonas his son.

I love the boy's threat of starving himself to death and the "There!" The petulance is so timeless. It was at times like this, when an ancient tatter suddenly spoke to me directly, that I missed you most, Helen. Lost time with a child can't be made up. It's a question that has always haunted me: was my work worth it? For all the joy of it, and that joy was real, were those hours and weeks and months worth it, when they kept me away from you? I always wanted to tell you things, instead spoke to an imaginary child in my head.

What's touching about these Oxyrhynchus writers is that nearly all of them were ordinary people talking about their ordinary lives. And there was tons of this stuff. Grenfell and Hunt filled up more than seven hundred tin chests with over half a million papyri fragments. God only knew what was still to be found, how many children missing their parents, how many parents missing their children.

"Those are the haven waters closest to Troy, with a handy harbour at the city's feet" (34–35): These waters have disappeared, filled in by the alluvial deposits of Troy's main rivers, the Scamander and the Símoïs. Today, between Capes Sigeum and Rhoeteum, there runs the edge of a rich plain intensively cultivated by modern Turkish farmers. But three thousand years ago, there was indeed a bay at the foot of Troy that faced north into the Hellespont, the old name for the Dardanelles, and into which ships coming from the Sea of Marmara and the Black Sea would have sailed easily. But the art of tacking into the wind was little known at the time, so during the navigable season, from May to October, the reverse journey up the Dardanelles was more problematic, to the benefit of the Trojans. There is no trace left of this proximal harbour.

"held on course by Boreas" (44): The Greek god of the North Wind.

"built a second harbour on their western shore" (48): A map will make the setting clear:

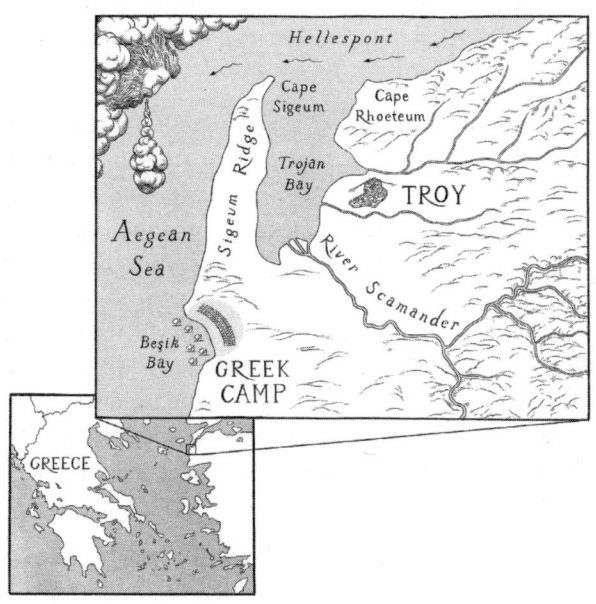

Despite the mythical embellishments—the hired Cyclops, the weaving gods—scholars and readers (Dennys, Kaiser, Bickmore, Byng, Heyward, Kanya-Forstner, Torrey, Tombere, Glusman, Kuipers, Foran, Swift, Swain, Slind, Theiss, Colomo, et al.) agree that Troy had an Aegean harbour, likely on what is now called Beşik Bay. Approximately eight kilometres from Troy, it would have been the city's main harbour, welcoming merchant ships from every corner of the Mediterranean, including Greek ships from directly across the Aegean, besides shipping out goods brought down the Hellespont but also delivered overland by the caravan routes of Asia Minor. Nor of this distal harbour, "a wonder of the world" (75), is there any trace left. These two harbours would have been the main source of Troy's Midas-like wealth (Midas was a vassal king of Troy, by the way).

"The gods themselves, Apollo and Hephaestus, wove all the moorings" (54–55): In addition to the incongruity of two mighty gods busying themselves with the dainty craft of weaving ropes while lesser beings do the heavy lifting of building a harbour, this is a somewhat strange match. In the Homeric tradition, Apollo strongly favours the Trojans, while Hephaestus, the blacksmith god, does not; he supports the Greeks. Perhaps he was well disposed toward

Troy in the halcyon days before the war. Being the god most concerned with crafts and trades, it makes sense that he would help with the building of Troy's Aegean harbour. He is also the husband of Aphrodite, who, as the goddess who bestowed Helen of Sparta on Paris, was the original backer of Troy. Nonetheless, he switches sides. Perhaps *The Psoad* harks to an older tradition in which Hephaestus rooted for the Trojans.

The reader might find the following list useful, for reference:

The Olympian gods on the Greek side:	The Olympian gods on the Trojan side:	Undecided:	Abstaining:
Hera	Aphrodite	Zeus	Demeter
Athena	Apollo		Hestia
Poseidon	Ares		Hades
Hephaestus	Artemis		
Hermes			

A house divided—but with admirable symmetry, as usual with the Ancient Greeks. Most gods pick a side, but a few sit it out. Unsurprisingly in a violent war epic, Demeter, the goddess of the harvest and fertility, is barely mentioned, and Hestia, the goddess of the home, is entirely absent. It makes sense that Zeus, the supreme god and final decider, should be ambivalent until the end. As for Hades, Lord of the Underworld, why should he choose sides? Either way, he does good business. More on him later.

"*'WHAT HARBOUR?' roared the king, cutting the merchant short*" (64): I considered the merchant Thromachis of Kos. He does something extremely unusual by Homeric standards: he speaks. More than that, he speaks at length and with knowledge. Meanwhile, Agamemnon, who appears to be the same ill-tempered, blundering commander he is in *The Iliad*, has clearly never seen the Trojan coast before and speaks only in questions ("These scrubby hills, that common beach? Are you sure?" 5), asking one of them twice ("What harbour?" 16 and 64); that is, he speaks from a position of ignorance. It's even worse than that for him:

> "... paying the Trojans, of course, for their hospi—"
> "WHAT HARBOUR?" roared the king, cutting the merchant short. (63–64)

To be heard by a common merchant, the King of Mycenae has not only to shout and repeat himself but to interrupt Thromachis.

In *The Iliad*, not a single commoner speaks (with one notable exception).

Homer's omniscient perspective closely aligns with the point of view of the Greek ruling class. It is an aristocratic perspective. Whereas here, a commoner speaks so much he practically filibusters.

On the number of ships that sink on the "porcupine's hackled back" (76): Well over sixty. In his Catalogue of Ships, Homer mentions some vessels, penteconters, being manned by 50 men (2.719), and others, early biremes, by 120 (2.510). Depending on the combination of ships, this would translate to losses of between 3,000 and 7,200 lives for sixty ships, if they had full crews, which is likely on a mission requiring forceful rowing at crosscurrent to break timber stakes anchored under water. Perhaps a number of the men were rescued. Whatever the loss, it would have been unexpected so early on, and disheartening.

"Psoas, the son of nobody" (85): From the rich sands of Oxyrhynchus, sailing in the same fleet as the merchant Thromachis of Kos and participating in the same action—the consequential vanishing of a harbour—Psoas reappeared, one late night in October in the Papyrology Work Room. There he was, next to the anonymous bard and a Dendran potter named Lakander. And whereas Psoas's first appearance was just a glimpse, no more than a man getting off a ship who is looking forward to a quick, lucrative war, this mention was far

more substantial. There is no talk in any other Trojan War tradition of a clever, elaborate ploy by the Trojans that costs the Greeks so many lives and ships upon their arrival. This was neither Homer—true or pseudo—nor the Epic Cycle. It was something else. It was confirmation that I had stumbled upon some unknown Trojan War story.

Right away the title for the epic came to me, an invention after the fact, as with the title of Homer's Trojan epic. *The Psoad* was born at that moment. I only had to find it now.

A thought occurred to me. I found my notebook and looked at the four lines from the Ashmolean ostraka:

> I am here because
> of Psoas of
> Midea son
> of nobody

I read them now in a different light. There was no insult here, after all. The speaker, that Mount Hymettos scribe and teacher, was "here" not because he was in a vengeful mood, but because he had heard, and been transported by, an epic about a son of nobody, and he wanted to praise him by a holy act of presence in a temple. This Ashmolean ostrakon, I now realized, was quite possibly the oldest fan letter in Western literature.

I had made a great discovery: I had unearthed an unknown Greek epic, or, at least, the hint of it. Being alone in the Work Room, I turned off the lights and sat there in the dark, in a daze. I felt stirring within me deep elation—and aching loneliness. My wife's last words at the airport still echoed in my head.

A daughter missed, a wife aggrieved, but a treasure to be found—how strangely my fate seemed to echo King Agamemnon's.

"Lakander, a potter from Dendra" (87): Another commoner who dares to speak, and once more with authority; in fact, Lakander does not just utter Psoas's idea that will save the Greek fleet, he hollers it (88). Odysseus seems in character, a deceitful fox, but strangely passive in this scene; he repeats what Lakander shouted ("He said it even louder" 92), but we don't actually hear him. The King of Ithaca is a silent parrot.

"theft is a king's right. (Talk to Epéüs about that.)" (93–94): In *The Iliad*, Epéüs appears as a fierce pugilist who wins the boxing match fought during the funeral games for Patroclus, and in *The Odyssey*, more to the point, he is mentioned as the master carpenter who builds the Trojan Horse, a conception

that is usually attributed to Odysseus. Psoas seems to imply here that Epéüs had a greater creative role than that of mere executor.

"while we sat" (99):

> Twenty ships we lost in this way, in no time,
> before our eyes, while we sat, as if at a play,
> many men in each—had the war even started? (98–100)

In the original, the staccato rhythm is pleasing, the incredulity of the Greeks perfectly summed up by the question at the end. Only there was something odd. I finally realized what it was: it was the verb "we sat" (καθεζόμεθα, *kathezometha* in Ancient Greek). As twenty ships are sinking, with all souls aboard drowning, wouldn't a man naturally jump up and lean over the waters, his arm extended in impotent rage and agony toward his dying mates? What kind of man would remain sitting?

The answer is simple: a man who has work to do. Work is important, indeed, essential. The kings and other bluebloods might be free to jump up, lean over, and extend their arms, but a working man, a *rowing* man, must remain seated. After all, the fleet has suddenly been ordered to stop its tremendous forward momentum (from minutes earlier: "we groaned with glad strain as we flew across the sea" 9). The ships must now hover in close proximity ("our thousand ships were pressing in" 83), which means the rowers have to focus on the boatswain's instructions, one moment rowing forward, the next backward. Is our bard a grunt sweating away in the galleys, an Ancient Greek Everyman gripping his oar as he cranes his neck to catch glimpses of the unfolding catastrophe?

"zigzagging to and fro" (101): The very words used by your teacher, Mrs. Adamson!

"Our ships never lulled our fear of water" (113): Swimming is a modern invention, hence the terror evoked by deep water in the ancient mind. In another tradition, when Jesus walks on water, an allegory on purity and sin, he plays on the same feeling. Sailing did little to allay the fear, since it was a hazardous activity in the Bronze Age, conducted with no maps or any other aids beyond rudimentary celestial navigation on ships that, by today's standards, were crude and lacking in resilience. The story of the river god Scamander, furious at Achilles for clogging his waters with the bodies of so many dead Trojans, pursuing the Greek hero across the Trojan plain in the form of a relentless wave, shared by both the Homeric and the Psoadic traditions, makes the point plainly: "Before water, the bravest man cowers" (118)—even a hero.

The animals mentioned (**passim**): The ships that "gallop like horses" (41) and the water "as solid as a bull" (115) are conventional metaphoric uses of well-known animals. Homer is full of them. The choices here are more offbeat. Who knew Greece had porcupines (76)? It is a curiosity of *The Psoad* that it abounds with a surprising variety of animals. You liked animals, too, Helen. They are dreams made flesh.

"Among them, standing proud and fierce, was Prince Mestor, one of the fifty sons of King Priam" (129–130): Who? Not Hector or Paris? Or some other famous Trojan hero, Aeneas or Sarpedon, Glaucus or Agenor?

A commoner from Midea, and now this obscure prince from Troy—what story was this?

The Arrival: The Good Country, the Walls of Troy

Said the King of Argolis, Diomédes,
"Go, scouts, go, up that way. Climb the seaside ridge.
Survey the enemy country, see and report.
Make sure the Trojans lie not in wait for us.
Beware: there are no bounds to their treachery."

It was then we noticed what was left undestroyed
by our foes, because of use in both directions,
whether winning or losing a battle:
a road from the harbour to the ridge above,
a road as one might see only in a city: 10
wide and ditched, the stones tightly fitted and level,
and scored, so that neither foot nor hoof might slip.
And this, on either side? *Ornamental shrubs?*

A road such as this, in the midst of scrub and bush,
was like a pearl necklace strung around a pig's neck.
We climbed the road, our shields up like a hand
protecting a flame on a windy day.

Atop the ridge, those of us who did not know,
yokel soldiers, gasped and stared in amazement.
The merchants who guided us smiled and nodded. 20

"Behold the sweeping plain of Ilios,"
said one merchant, deep-voiced. "There is your foe,
a city more songed than even Babylon.
There, before your eyes, is King Priam's Troy,
the favoured destination of the world,
begetter of roads, port of all sea routes,
capital of three seas, agent of three empires,
the vast kingdom that needs no land because
all wealth flows to it, like rivers to the sea.

Consider sacred Troy's watery wealth. 30
The Æsépus, yonder, is the border river
of Priam's kingdom beyond which his subjects
care not to live, as if it were the Styx,
and to many of you it will be the Styx
as you cross it on your way to Hades.
Yes, many of you are fated to die.
And before your eyes, greatest of them all,
flow the holy Scamander and Símoïs.
There are seven more, can you believe it?
Ilios is so rich it flaunts ten rivers, 40
while our lands are as dry as camel shit.
This is good country, friends. Figs, grapes, oil and honey,
fruit trees of every kind, fields that grow all grains,
others that feed cattle and Troy's famed horses.
More wine than water, the best artisans.
You saw the coastline, drab and uninviting.
It is like a plain box hiding a treasure.

This is no ordinary land. It is a womb,
and all round you will see the life born of it.
The soil here will turn your tent poles into trees. 50
Stand too long and your sandals will grow roots.
Is it any wonder Priam has fifty sons?
This is good country—have I said that already?
And you haven't seen Troy itself, have you?
There is no city like it. Paved streets throughout.
Every palace and temple of marble rosy
and white, with windows that frame the horizon,
but also two-storied brick houses for all,
with water supplied by clay pipes, so clever,
and balconies that look upon gardens and ponds. 60
So many bathhouses and grand theatres.
Everywhere you turn, clean lines and right angles,
colourful fabrics and artful objects.
It's a wonder the gods of Olympus
don't choose to live in sacred Ilios.

And all this is but a stage, so take a seat.
Wait till you hear the story—Troy has it all.
A fortified city, a seaside encampment,
ships, chariots, horses, and best of all,
sure to fire up your loins, men in uniform, 70
mortal enemies who are willing to grab
every kind of weapon: sword, spear, arrow, rock.
Men taunting, men shouting, men fighting, men dying.
Great battles in the field during the day,
fantastic orgies in the big tents at night.
Handsome men, beautiful women, lovely children,
exotic tribes, priests and seers as needed.
Plundered cities, blazing fires, piles of loot.
Stirring speeches, sharp exchanges, breathless whispers.
Dice games, funeral pyres, wrestling matches, 80
archery contests, chariot races.
All the violence you want, need, and love
in every possible form—suicides, murders,

duels, skirmishes, melees, full-out battles—
bringing you deaths gurgling, gory, and gruesome,
blood everywhere and everyone screaming.
Wisdom, folly, heroism, cowardice,
devotion, treachery, cruelty, tenderness.
Pleas, rebuffs, anger, forgiveness, sighs, shouts.
Heartbreak to split a stone, love to make you weep. 90
And you can really settle into the story.
It goes on and on, for so many episodes,
with more twists in the plot than a million snakes.
You can even join in, if you want, for fun—
help kill men, increase suffering, that sort of thing—
or you can just sit back and watch, up to you.
But take note: over there, to the southeast,
Troy's realm is bounded by Mount Ida. Atop,
Zeus, king of gods, resides there oftentimes.
Warring at his feet, best not to arouse his ire." 100

The Trojan enemy wasn't hiding.
He was marching up the road ahead of us,
hauling homeward our fallen men's arms and armour.
Nor was his city hidden. Great Zeus, what a sight!
Troy lay open and displayed across the plain,
plain to see, a brilliant hive of temples,
palaces, houses, markets, streets and squares.
Next to the citadel, to the south and east,
upon a broad apron of sloping ground,
lay the lower town, and just as the features   110
of a high mountain can be seen from below,
just so, from the Sigeum Ridge where we stood,
could the features of Ilios be seen
from outside its walls, a city living its life,
men working, women tending, children playing.
As we descended from the seaside ridge,
Troy's walls loomed ever higher—and what walls were these?

"Refreshed and repainted to welcome you,"
said the deep voice. "This is one of their talents."

The walls of Troy, so high, so bright, so final, 120
built by the hands of Apollo and Poseidon,
they say. The godly touch was plain to see.
Most impressive of all were the mosaics,
vaster than the sails that had brought us to Troy.
Such beautiful images on so grand a scale
were unknown to us, showing gods and kings of such
proportions that had they deigned to reach down,
they could have picked up one of our warships.
Those facing water stood proud and martial,
set for war, while those facing land lay in gardens, 130
garlanded with flowers, cups of wine in hand,
reposing to the music of lutes and lyres,
or hunting stags and lions, arrows flying.
About them mortals worked the giving earth,

ploughing deep furrows with teams of oxen,
casting wide nets into teeming waters,
reaping from the earth, reaping from the sea.
And we noticed: their men, women, and children—
they dressed like us, they worked like us, they played like us,
and they slept like us and they died like us.   140
Every tool, every field, every weave, every cot,
the same, the same. Every cart, every hut,
every boat, every bier, the same, the same.
As you walked around Troy, so you walked around life.
Every season showed, of man and the earth,
summer, winter, sun, rain, morning, noon, and night,
babies wriggling, women dancing, men weeping,
they like us, we like them, the same, the same.
We looked at these chameleon walls wide-eyed,
marvelling, as if we had come as guests.   150

But we had come as foes. We attacked the walls.

For years, the telltale sign of an Argive
who had fought at Troy, a sorry trophy,
was a handful of colourful tesserae
from its ravaged walls, picked up after battle.
We all brought them home, these hard-come-by glints,
until you could find them hawked in any market,
some, if you wished, at a premium, see here,
splashed with Hector's very blood (seller's honour).

We gave up destroying Troy's godly walls,   160
because they were beyond mortal destruction,
only painted its feet with our red blood.
After that, through the seasons and the years,
we watched the sun and the rain do their work.
The gods and kings became faded and chipped,
although the Trojans, in the midst of battles
and during truces, at all times, lowered craftsmen
in baskets held by ropes, with shields on their backs,

to touch up the mosaics, to rile us.

It was the eyes they worked on, we noticed,   170
always the eyes, so that throughout the war,
for ten long years, the eyes of gods and kings
glared at us from the walls of sacred Troy.

"like a pearl necklace strung around a pig's neck" (15): How curiously this is echoed in Matthew 7:6:

> Do not give what is holy to dogs; and do not throw your pearls before swine, or they will trample them under foot and turn and maul you.

The biblical metaphor is muddled. The animals' reactions to the unexpected offerings are strangely conflated. Do dogs trample? Do pigs maul? And why would they be angry in the face of the holy and pearls, a peculiar pairing? The Psoadic image is far sharper, with that crystalline clarity one finds again and again in Greek epic, in Homer above all. One can well imagine a pig proudly displaying its glossy pearl necklace, pink with self-satisfaction, as its Nero-like Trojan owner looks on. And roads are long and thin and wrap around a landscape like a necklace wraps around a neck—the image works that way, too, in the unconscious connection between the two objects being compared. Could it be that the image of a bejewelled pig in a lost Greek epic struck the ancient imagination and lingered, until centuries later Matthew mangled it? Or since Matthew here is bearing witness to the Sermon on the Mount, until Jesus mangled it?

Such a difference in style is to be expected. Both texts speak with authority, but the authority of the Gospels relies on its claim to truth, while that of *The*

Iliad relies on its power to captivate. Natural, then, that the delivery of the latter would be smoother and more beguiling.

Speaking of mangling, this fragment was tenuously collated from hundreds of separate papyrus finds, perhaps bringing together elements that once stood apart, hence the surprising leap from a fresh arrival at Troy to an encapsulation of what is to happen in years to come, and the description of the city's fresh walls and then their immediate surface destruction before the Greeks have even fought a battle. And the ecphrasis of the walls in lines 125–148 is a detailed bird's-eye view implying a slow, attentive walk around the entire fortified city, and this, when the newly arrived observer has just reached a ridge miles away.

At least this stitched fragment delivers all the bits about the wall in one go. With this diorama of Troy in mind, we now have a setting in which to place the characters of the tale and watch the unfolding events, how blindness led wide-eyed men to their doom.

"Behold the sweeping plain of Ilios" (21): Ilios was another Greek name for Troy, whence the noun and adjective Ilian, the adjective Iliadic, and the title of Homer's epic.

"So what's *The Iliad* about, Daddy?" you asked, your face shining brightly on my phone. Seeing you and talking to you every few days always lifted my spirits.

I was gratified that you were asking, Helen. You saw my smile. Homer, after all, is truly interesting, even to a child. I was sitting on my bed in my residence at Oxford, you were sitting on yours at home, but at that moment, as we were talking, I felt we were in the same room.

"It's about a bitter dispute between two big men, King Agamemnon, the top general of the Greek forces at Troy, and Achilles, the greatest of the Greek fighters. Though they're on the same side, they can't stop being angry at each other. *The Iliad* is about the terrible consequences of that anger."

"Do they shout and fight?"

"They certainly do. Achilles comes close to ki—"

"So it's like you and Mommy."

"Well, no, I wouldn't say that."

"You and Mommy are always shouting and fighting."

"No, no. We just have our differences sometimes."

"Are there any girls in the story?"

There are. I told you about the women in *The Iliad*. There is Helen, of course, at the heart of the war, its root and flower, the beginning and the end of it. There's Hecuba, Queen of Troy, and there's Andromache, Hector's beloved wife. Two other women, Chryseïs and Briseïs, are the cause of the fight between Agamemnon and Achilles. A woman is the first victim of the war—Iphigenia, sacrificed by Agamemnon, her father, to pacify a goddess, Artemis—and a woman is the last victim of the war, Polyxena. And when the Greeks desecrate her temple, Athena—before you interrupted me.

"Do the goddesses actually *do* anything?"

"Oh, absolutely. Hera intervenes all the time in the war. She pulls tricks on Zeus. Aphrodite actually appears on the battlefield. And early on in the epic, Athena grabs Achilles by the hair, spins him round, and tells him not to kill Agamemnon. It's a great scene. I hope you read Homer one day, Helen, when you're ready. His epics are the Bible and Google of the Greeks, the stories that made them Greeks. They're full of grand moments and colourful details, delivered in language that's as clear as sunlight. But listen, thanks for asking about my work. I really appreciate it. And do you really think—"

"Oh! Mommy's brought out the ice cream. Bye!"

[*meeting ended*]

"as dry as camel shit" (41): Camels are not native to Greece, but the surprise here does not lie with the odd animal—we already know to expect those in *The Psoad*. It is a merchant who is speaking (22), and any merchant who had been to North Africa would have encountered camels. The surprise is the coarse image, in the original κόπρος, *kopros*, "shit". Homer, for all the violence of his tales,

is remarkably tame of tongue. Which is strange, no? Greek epic was originally delivered orally, and while coarseness on the page can jump out and jar, it lends itself to speech, where its emotional tone can be calibrated to land just right on the ear, bracingly realistic or profanely humorous, rather than just crude. And let's not forget, let's get real here: a war is on. Since when have soldiers at war been mealy-mouthed?

I mulled over this line. It was my first hint as to the identity of the bard of *The Psoad*.

"This is good country" (42): What I would say of my residence room. Manorial as Holywell Ford appeared on the outside, it was drably modern and functional on the inside, and as well-worn as an old leather shoe by the generations of graduate students who had lived there before my time. It provided the minimal necessities of domestic life: a narrow bed, a desk, a small sofa, a hot plate and a small refrigerator—a cell-like haven perfect for sustained reflection. Its windows graced me nearly daily with a view of Magdalen's herd of deer and, somewhat less enchanting, its herd of goats. The first looked like the Oxford University one might imagine—poised, deliberate, regal—while the second, when they were bleating, sounded like students barfing after a night of drinking.

The door of the wardrobe in my room had a full-length mirror, speckled with age, with a patch from the white underlay of a sticker on which one could still make out the words "Irn-Bru"—a trace of a former resident, presumably Scottish. I looked at my resulting mottled image. My inner self was rankled. I felt like an impostor here at Oxford, a perhaps not uncommon feeling among students in a place so freighted with history. And I had no money, which did not help. Everything here was more expensive than I had anticipated, and I was loath to ask Gail for help. I counted my every pence, avoiding the cafés where other students endlessly lounged, eating only at the prescribed times in the prescribed cafeterias.

At least the ideas at Oxford were free. And this feeling of not fitting in also allowed the possibility of renewal, did it not? The ship is about to leave and the captain is calling out to you: "Come, come!"

Do you stay or do you go? What do you do, son of nobody?

"Is it any wonder Priam has fifty sons?" (52): Homer also credits Priam with fifty sons, while Virgil adds a hundred daughters. Even on the scale of epic exaggeration, this is extravagant. It stands in stark contrast to the pinched birth rate of the Greek heroes. How many children does Agamemnon have? One son, Orestes, and three daughters. How many children does Menelaus

have? One girl, Hermione, and one illegitimate son, Megapenthes. How many children does Odysseus have? One son, Telemachus, with Penelope, and three with Circe. How many children does Achilles have? One, Neoptolemus. And so on. It all speaks to the boundless wealth of Troy.

"You can even join in, if you want, for fun—help kill men, increase suffering, that sort of thing—or you can just sit back and watch, up to you" (94–96): It is a merchant who is speaking, but displaying such gusto, knowledge, and foresight, he is more likely a god, perhaps Zeus himself, hence his deep voice (twice pointed out: 22 and 119), his knowledge of the misery that lies ahead for the Greeks, and his warning not to bother the neighbour on Mount Ida ("Warring at his feet, best not to arouse his ire" 100). But in Homer, as in other religious traditions, mortals usually see through the human disguises of gods, especially when they sound like James Earl Jones or Morgan Freeman.

And to whom is this merchant/god speaking? Seemingly the Greek men. But he could also be speaking to his fellow Olympians, inviting them to binge-watch the war with him, even "join in" (which would explain the "*help* kill men", since Greek gods usually kill mortals through other mortals, and not directly). Even more intriguing a notion, perhaps it is the bard speaking here, in which case the invitation to listeners either to spectate or to participate alludes to the openness of the oral tradition, how it was in creative flux, constantly being co-created by attentive bards and their attentive listeners. A story is a never-ending invention.

"*Next to the citadel, to the south and east, upon a broad apron of sloping ground, lay the lower town*" (108–110): Homer makes no mention of the lower town; in fact, he makes no mention of any urban detail to do with Troy. The lower town would have been the city's economic engine, where its celebrated artisans plied their various trades in their vast workshops. Troy, it bears reminding, was the largest city in all of southeastern Europe and western Asia Minor at the time. A metropolis. A sight indeed to impress the Greeks.

"*The walls of Troy, so high, so bright, so final*" (120): And so fictitious. It's a common trick of storytellers, to lay it on thick. The walls that the visitor can see today would credibly have the effect described by the bards only if the Greeks were three inches tall. Great Troy is now an unimpressive mound, its mythical might so diminished that even its name was swept away, changed to Hisarlik. Most tourists who come to this part of the Aegean coast of Turkey, near the entrance to the Dardanelles, save their awe for the memorials of Gallipoli across the water, preferring the site that was the crucible of the Australian and New Zealander character over the one that was the crucible of the

Greek. The dolled-up remains of Troy earn no more than a quick, indifferent gander, eliciting from the average visitor no deeper reaction than "Really? Is that it?"

This brings up a key question: to what degree are these ancient songs history, and to what degree, fiction? There is no easy answer. We have no historical proof for the existence of any of the protagonists or antagonists of the Trojan War—not for Helen, Paris, Agamemnon, Menelaus, Odysseus, Achilles, Patroclus, Diomédes, Ajax, Priam, Hector, Hecuba, Cassandra, Andromache, or any others—nor do we have any solid proof of any specific war between the Ancient Greeks and the Trojans. In *The Iliad*, the mythical, the current, and the invented are blended with the factually minor (a boar's tusk helmet, for example). Homer's *Iliad* is a searing vision rather than a witnessed event. Later writers, both Greek (Euripides, Aeschylus, Sophocles, Herodotus, Thucydides, and others) and, centuries later, Roman (Livy, Ovid, Virgil, Quintus of Smyrna, to name just a few), expanded the story—all of it further yarn, of course—until we have the fantastical Trojan War as we know it today. This seminal event of antiquity, along with the other foundational stories of the great past—*Gilgamesh*, the Bible, the Gospels, and the like—all belong to the verdant realm of fiction (hence their power), with only a few, thread-like tendrils reaching out to verifiable facts.

But taking it all back, Mycenaean civilization really did collapse around 1200 BCE, right after the purported Trojan War, plunging the Greeks into their very own, centuries-long Dark Ages. Wars do that: they cause empires to fall and times to change. So if the bards were spouting fiction, their stories, in the absence of actual history, very nicely explained the end of a people, an age, a civilization, and laid the foundation for what followed. Their stories did something surprising: they made the facts unnecessary. Or, to put it another way, their stories became facts, as solid to build upon. This synergy makes sense. History, however true, needs interpreting, and fiction, however invented, arises from life and reflects it.

With these old stories, to make them meaningful, to feed off them, we must take them at their word. So we take epic exaggeration seriously, as we do Gospel gravity, otherwise there is nothing to take.

The tools of critical analysis applied to Troy, then, like those applied to the life and sayings of Jesus, the labour of exegesis, are therefore inherently problematic. Each tool holds up more or less, is debatable, disputable, refutable, can be held to be a matter of conjecture and opinion. Using them creates as much a work of fiction as of restoration. But the approach is tenable, since the true poet's only invention is the truth—as here, with the walls of Troy.

A siege naturally involves a lot of waiting around, especially one with no technological means to break it, as was the case with Troy, and prolonged waiting is very trying. Waiting gives no direction, no means to act, forces upon one unwanted ruminations, leads to boredom, and builds up frustrations. Waiting is an incubator of wild ideas and unwarranted rage, hence the violence that can arise when it finally ends.

Waiting fascinates the ancient and modern minds because to learn how to live is to learn how to wait, how to deal with the sand as it falls through the hourglass. We must therefore take the astonishing walls of Troy not as a feat of Bronze Age architecture but as a symbol of the human condition. Like us, Psoas was born to wait before a wall.

"the eyes of gods and kings glared at us" (172–173): Ice cream for you, silence for me. Gail chose not to talk to me, once more. Since I'd left Canada, she and I had talked only a handful of times, always briefly on her way to handing the phone to you or to hanging up. She was in a meeting, she said, she was cooking supper, she said, she was on her way out the door, she said. And now you comparing us to enraged Agamemnon and Achilles.

Anger, that poison, then as now.

The Layout of the Ships (bis)

Between the mighty ships of the two great kings,
Zeus-like Agamemnon's one hundred sea-borne
fortresses, and those of his brother, fierce
Lord Menelaus's sixty grand warships,
rested on the sands the fear-striking vessels
of god-feared Lord Diomédes, eighty in all.
And next to these, on the Agamemnon side,
lying in wait like a lion about to pounce,
crouched the forty proud ships of Midea,
on which arrived Psoas, the son of nobody.　　　　　　　　10
"What a magnificent sight, our armada of
one thousand one hundred and eighty-six warships!"
said he. "We will make good of our time here.
To take from the rich Trojans, what a dream."

The Layout of the Ships (title): In all logic, this is where this fragment should appear in the narrative. Though the location of the Greek encampment is not mentioned in *The Psoad* (or *The Iliad*, for that matter), it is probable that after their disastrous landing on the Aegean coast of the Troad, Agamemnon and his forces eventually made their way around Cape Sigeum and set up in Trojan Bay, likely on its southwestern edge, their backs protected by the Sigeum Ridge, their enemies lying before them across the bay.

So here, rather than there:

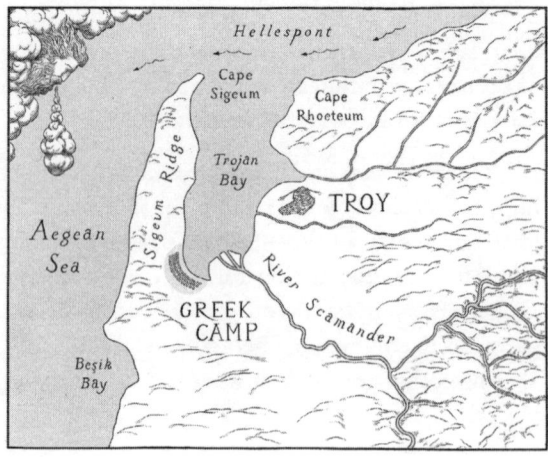

If that is so, then Psoas's proud tone is odd. The Greeks, after their first misadventure, would no longer have 1,186 ships. Surely, by now, the shine of their arrival would have started to wear off. The scene seems to serve only one purpose: to introduce the hero, a commoner, as he strides off his ship, admires the Greek fleet, and looks forward to his good fortune.

"what a dream" (14): So true. I threw myself at my work. Troy, in all its ancient glory—those walls, that world—rose up before my eyes, and, like Psoas, I hoped to take from the rich Trojans.

How Men Fought: The Hero and the Ordinary Man

Other men—Psoas among them—fought more loosely,
carrying two spears and a trusty sword,
with space around in which to kill or be killed.

If a phalanx was a herd of wildebeest,
strong by size, then a hero was a lone lion.
Have you heard of Achilles? No? Well, you will soon.
Have you heard of Hector? No? Well, you will soon.
Against a hero, there was nothing to be done,
no safety, no reprieve, no mercy, no chance.
Tired of petty prey that only fled before him,   10
a hero might turn and stare at a foe's phalanx,
say a word to his men and point at it
with his sword. Sometimes just this would be enough:

the phalanx would fall apart and sixty men—
sixty hardened warriors—would flee pell-mell,
like rabbits, only to be run down and slaughtered.
But even if the formation stayed put,
every eye focused hard, the commander
holding a tight rein on his men, still then
the outcome was the same: sixty dead men.　　　　　　　20
How is this possible? How can one man
and his few helpers take on *sixty* fighters?
But it was even more far-fetched than that.
Who said the hero's helpers helped the hero?
They didn't. I know this because I saw it
with my own eyes, heard it with my own ears,
how one hero would massacre a whole phalanx.
Be it Achilles or Hector, it was the same:

At a run, the hero would throw himself
at the phalanx with deathless abandon.   30
A mighty throw of his ash spear would fell a foe
and turn his fallen shield into an open gate.
Through this breach the hero charged, taking advantage
of the dread and awe among his opponents.
Now in their midst, he turned and swung his shield,
deflecting spears and swords, knocking men over,
using as shields his foes, who took blows meant for him
or prevented others from getting sword-close,
while in his other hand his sword spun faster
than a chariot wheel behind galloping steeds.   40

The hero fought, while his enemies jostled.
The hero did not stride or march, he danced.
Leaping and spinning in circle upon circle,
he travelled as if upon a dance floor.
A hero hacking his way through enemies—

---

the chaos, the armour-clattering death of men—
and a hero dancing of an evening—
the flutes, the lyres, the drums, the light of fires:
it was much the same thing, a show of such grace
that his opponents yielded as much to it 50
as to the actual blows that killed them.
The more the hero spun and leapt and whirled
to the jarring, clanging music of death,
the more his foes around him were spellbound.
Oh, the screaming, the gurgling, the gasping!
Such were the wondrous motions of the hero,
and, no doubt, the protection of the gods.
And so one hero defeated sixty men.
Such a hero was Prince Mestor of Troy.

What is it that makes a hero a hero? 60
His costly weapons and armour play a part,
made to measure by the most skilled blacksmiths

who learned their trade from Hephaestus himself.
His lengthy training, too, since he was a child.
And you have to imagine his splendid dress,
and his long hair, like the mane of a lion.
But no matter the gear, no matter the garb,
it all comes down to the fierce light in his eyes,
kindled by the roaring fire of battle.
Compared to the hero, the ordinary man 70
has no more character than a shadow,
and before the light, shadows fall away.
Such a hero was Prince Mestor of Troy.

The ordinary man, just before battle,
has an ashen face and sways on his feet.
His breathing is noisy, quick, and shallow,
and from the pumping of the veins in his neck
you know his heart is jumping about his chest.
Suddenly he bends over and vomits,

which brings him no relief. He stands again,　　　　　　　　　80
covered in a glaze of sweat, his teeth chattering.
His gaze is fixed, yet he seems to see nothing.
When you drape your arm over his shoulder,
you realize he is trembling all over.
He is consumed with dread, as if a Cyclops
were chewing him whole, and the main ingredient
of the monster's saliva, that which breaks down
the man's bones and melts his guts, is a herb called fear.
He stands next to you, the ordinary man,
crushed by this Cyclops's teeth, macerated　　　　　　　　　90
in the dissolving juices of his mouth,
and he is wet—drenched—*saturated* with terror.
A poor man, his gear is shoddy and ill-fitting.
His helmet chafes, and in summer it is hot,
the cause of the sweat that pours into his eyes,
and in winter it brings his cold head no comfort.
And always it restricts his view, muffles his ears.

His armour and greaves rub, his shield is heavy,
his spear and his sword are ungainly tools.
At all times he is in negotiations100
with his equipment, seeking compromise.
When he moves, he is a clanking wagon,
all his parts knocking against each other.
The ordinary man, before he can deal
with his enemy, must first deal with himself.
He is told that with a little luck and pluck,
he can upgrade his kit, taking from a dead man.
Will he be lucky? Will he be plucky?
He marches off, glancing back at you one last time,
and you are fearfully certain of his fate,110
that he will not see the end of this day
but will be killed by the first foe he meets,
putting up no fight, dying with modesty.
Such a poor man was Psoas of Midea.

Yet that day you might also see the opposite.
You might see on the field the ordinary man
battling the many foes surrounding him,
killing man after man, his face impassive,
his actions quick, his intent precise and deadly,
just as you might see the hero fleeing   120
like a hare pursued by dogs, face white with fear.
Such is the glory and dread of war, in which
fear lives with joy like husband lives with wife.

"*If a phalanx was a herd of wildebeest . . . then a hero was a lone lion*" (4–5): There were lions in Greece and Asia Minor at the time, but certainly no wildebeest, which, as far as is known, have never ranged north of the Sahara. How did gnus make it into a Greek epic? Did a Mycenaean trader actually travel all the way down the Nile and then some leagues more overland and see for himself the interaction between lions and wildebeest? If so, this allusion in *The Psoad* is the only historical trace of such a distant Mycenaean voyage into Africa. Otherwise, it was perhaps just word of mouth, a trader at the mouth of the Nile who was attentive to stories of marvels and wonders from upriver. Why the Psoadic bard didn't fall back on lions and sheep, the usual Homeric trope, an image that would have been far more familiar to his audience, is impossible to determine. I would venture the guess of wilful exoticism on the bard's part.

"*Have you heard of Achilles? No? Well, you will soon. Have you heard of Hector? No? Well, you will soon*" (6–7): To say that these two lines jumped out at me is an understatement. They are genuinely startling. Because if the bard is asking these questions, it implies he is telling his story to people who are not familiar with it, who have never heard of the heroes whose fame endures to this day. Clearly, something dramatic of a military nature happened in northwest

Asia Minor at the end of the Bronze Age, and bards started singing about it. But before they could tell stirring stories of known heroes, they first had to set the scene. This is how men fought, this is how some distinguished themselves. The fragment above must therefore have been sung not long after the end of the Trojan War, while audiences were still learning about the characters who fought in it and coming to understand the nature and magnitude of the event. That would date this song of Troy, or at least the germ of it, to before the Greek Dark Ages and make it one of the oldest accounts on record.

Dating the Trojan War is problematic. Since we have no evidence there ever was an actual ten-year Trojan War as sung by the bards, it's not surprising that we also don't know when that war might have taken place. Some traditional dates for the end of the Trojan War are 1250 and 1184 BCE, but these are speculations, with no basis in attestable facts. It's very much like the birth year of Jesus. Was he born in 6 BCE? In 4? The year 0? A few years later?

We also don't know who Homer was, just as we don't know who the Gospel writers were, historically. Homer is a nom de plume for a full stop at the end of a long sentence of unknown bards. Whatever images of Homer the reader may have seen, likely that of a blind man with a full beard staring upwards in the wild transports of inspiration, these are, like images of a lithe, understatedly handsome young man with a beard meant to represent Jesus (what's with all the beards?), fictions. Jesus was sharply one, while Homer was a blur of many, and both have been the subject of unceasing attention, our fixed gaze, but for all that we don't know what either looked like or, more importantly, who exactly conveyed their stories.

It is curious how two stories that have so changed history are so very hard to place *in* history.

"*his long hair, like the mane of a lion*" (66): A cliché now, a striking image then.

***The ordinary man's fear* (74–92):** Was the bard making a general observation about the effect of war on the foot soldier, or was it specific to the Trojan War? I'm inclined to think the second. There must have been something exceptional about the war. There is clear evidence to this effect. Most obviously, the Trojan War led to the disintegration of Mycenaean civilization. But there's something more: we're still talking about it. In this, the Trojan War is, once again, like Jesus of Nazareth. There were Jewish messiahs aplenty during the Roman occupation of Palestine, each making his wild claims before being killed off by the Roman authorities. All these Simon bar Kokhbas have vanished from general discourse and remain meaningful today only to historians of the period or residents of the locality. But whether it was a matter of divinity or extraordinary charisma, people are still talking about Jesus. And so too with the Trojan War: in a time of incessant conflicts, it stood out. And why would that be if not because of its terrifying appetite for the lives of men? In Dares the Phrygian's *History of the Fall of Troy*, a supposedly personal account from a Trojan priest of Hephaestus (who is mentioned in *The Iliad*), Dares speaks of 886,000 casualties on the Greek side and 676,000 on the Trojan side, excluding the casualties of foreign allies. Of course, this is hyperbole based on no verifiable evidence. But the very exaggeration speaks of lasting shock.

If Jesus is about life eternal, then Troy is about death eternal.

The ordinary man's fear (74–92): New love is always in a rush, pressed on by hope and worry. Was Gail interested in me, or was she just being friendly? When her phone pinged and she turned to it, was she expressing boredom at being with me (she was turning on Do Not Disturb)? When she delayed answering my text, was she trying to put me off (she was in the shower)? When she was not there at the appointed time and place, was she telling me to stop, to just *stop* (her brother broke his arm tripping over a laundry basket and she had to bring him to the hospital, where she left him to race to meet me)? Love is a swirl, a tumult, an explosion.

"Such a poor man was Psoas of Midea" (114): And yet, among the thousands of foot soldiers at Troy, this ordinary man stood out. What did Psoas do that he would not be dispatched with the gift of one of Homer's obituaries (see footnote *"What a magnificent sight, our armada of one thousand one hundred and eighty-six warships!"*, page 36), but placed at the centre of his very own epic? Did he surprise the bard by returning from battle, day after day? Did other men, Greek and Trojan, start to see "the fierce light in his eyes" (68)? But if Psoas was a hero in the making, why had his epic vanished?

*Prince Mestor and the Son of Nobody
    Meet for the First Time*

They stood, blood-spattered and weary both of them,
there, not far from the banks of the Scamander.
The tide of war had moved away a little
and they were resting not far from each other.
Each man saw the other, and their gazes locked.

Said one, high-born, to the other, low-born,
"Who are you, dog-face? Where lies the land that raised you?"

Said the other, "I am Psoas of Midea."

Said the other, "My foe, then, a little one."

Replied the son of nobody, "Who are you?" 10

Replied the other, "Who am I? To you,
Psoas of Midea, I am the sun.
Before you stands Prince Mestor of sacred Troy,
one of the fifty sons of King Priam,
which means that before this day is over
I will return to a city the likes of which
you have never seen, nor can even imagine.
I live in a city of treasure and trust.
Every day I hear the music of lyres and looms,
of horses and hammers, of dice games and dye vats. 20
Most precious of all, the heart of my city,
I will hear and see my wife and children.
Whereas you, dog, if you die today, you'll have been
away from your wife and children for ten long years.
For what? Your name will have no glory to it.
Your ugly children won't remember you—

they've grown to be weaklings in your absence—
and your chicken-headed wife has forgotten you.
Enough. Already this day have I killed five foes,
though the sun is not yet midway to noon, 30
so move off, son of nobody, move off,
unless you wish to be my sixth victim."
Psoas of Midea did as he was told,
he moved off, though it did occur to him
that already that day he too had killed five foes,
though the sun was not yet midway to noon.
Much did he dwell on the unpleasant words
Prince Mestor of Troy had uttered to him.

"*I live in a city of treasure and trust*" (18): Presumably the abundance of well-shared treasure leads to trust, which in turn leads to a willingness to make more treasure, so we have here a statement on the Trojans' equitable social relations. The sentiment is echoed in the line "I hear the music of lyres and looms, of horses and hammers, of dice games and dye vats" (19–20), in which items of leisure are paired with items of industry. If it seems strange, even unlikely, that a prince, one at the apex of a highly stratified Bronze Age society, should notice the tools and the wider benefit of the work of low-born artisans ("a city the likes of which you have never seen" 16–17)—is it any stranger, any more unlikely, than Jesus, an illiterate, impoverished tradesman from an oppressed minority, preaching lessons of refined love to one and all?

"*I live in a city of treasure and trust*" (18): Gail was interested in me! Love never walks—it strides, it leaps, it flies. In the arched doorway of a building, after a night out, the snow swirling around us, the moment was at hand, to be seized: I reached, Gail consented, we kissed. A small embryo of warmth in a vastness of cold. The spark in her eyes, the kindle in my heart, the fire in the night.

"*I live in a city of treasure and trust*" (18): The exhilaration of getting undressed with her, she taking off her clothes, me taking off mine, five items for her, four for me. We met with our eyes wide open, crossing borders with the breathless excitement of travelers. How perfect, those university student beds, meant for one, ideal for two. Gail was a country I never wanted to leave.

"I live in a city of treasure and trust" (18): Her pile of clothes on the floor, like the cover of a book. The words we shared while lying with each other, like the pages of a good novel. Gail was a book I never wanted to close.

"I live in a city of treasure and trust" (18): The exquisite sweetness of animal proximity, each of us a chameleon matching the other's mood. Gail was an adaptation I never wanted to be done with.

"Much did he dwell on the unpleasant words Prince Mestor of Troy had uttered to him" (37–38): What do you do when it's just not working, no matter how many times you both say sorry after the meandering, unproductive arguments and try again? When you've read the relationship books and seen the counselor and all that, and still you fall into the same glum routine of bearing it one day at a time? How do you rebuild a city whose treasure and trust lie in ruins?

The Death of Elanthius

Standing before Troy's walls, our kings found the weak point.
We would leave the high-walled acropolis
—King Priam's splendid and eternal city—
for later, and start with the tucked-away
lower town—Priam's craven and greedy purse.
The merchants had told us its outer wall
was a low timber palisade, only that.

We looked left and right in fearful wonder.
Where was this timber palisade, "only that"?
Around their lower town, for over three leagues,   10
our Trojan foes had dressed their breast of wood
with an armour of sturdy mud-brick wall,
with battlements atop and stone-footed towers,

with on the ground a triple row of sharp stakes
and below a deep ditch hewn into the rock.

Do all the towns in these lands have defences
such as these? All the merchants shook their heads.
No, they had never seen anything like it.
This was all new, they said, this was all new.
Who had ever heard of such involved efforts   20
to protect artisans, slaves, and barbarians?

No matter. At our kings' command, we attacked,
fools that we were. We lost men, years, and heart,
dying daily to win a potter's vacant house,
a smith's empty workshop, a bare dorm room for slaves,
fighting not in the light of an open plain,
standing tall, but crouched in the shadows and corners
of an endless maze of brick walls, fearful mice.

None were left in the lower town but a few,
and one of these was old Elanthius, 30
whom the son of nobody found next to a wall,
sitting at a table, his gaze and breathing calm.
He was not hiding, though war was all around them—
running and shouting, fire, soot, and wreckage.
Elanthius sat with water and food, waiting.

Said Psoas, "Who are you? Why are you still here?"

Replied the calm man, "My name is Elanthius.
I am a carpenter from Phrygia,
but Troy has been my home for many years,
the source of all my wealth and happiness. 40
Sit a moment, take this chair, just for a few words.
Tell me, how many legs do your tables have?"

Replied Psoas, "In my homeland? They have three legs."

Said Elanthius, "Of course. A lesser people.
A table with three legs will be stable enough
on any floor, at the cost of being level.
To have level tables, you need level floors.
So what happens on the festive occasion
when many are invited to share a meal,
the table as a symbol of unity? 50
You can bring stools and tables together,
one table tilting this way, another that way,
a plane of dislocated surfaces.
But watch, soon, by wine or sober blunder,
a table is upset, then another,
and soon you have an angry mess. Better to sit
away from each other in your chill megarons,
glowering from your triangular tables.
With table dynamics like that, is it any
wonder you Argives are such a prickly, 60
ill-tempered lot? I was the best table-maker

in all of Ilios. Look and count, man.
How many legs do you see on this table?"

Replied Psoas, counting, "I see four legs."

"And what shape is this four-legged table?"

Replied Psoas, "It is shaped like a rectangle."

"Indeed. And as level as the horizon.
To my best customers, Trojan and Hittite,
I offered inlays—ivory, mother-of-pearl,
what you want, even gold, top quality   70
all of it, the wood and the build, guaranteed.
But for you lot? Why build well what won't last long?
Any ruffian can buy a good table,
but you can't level a bad floor. I doubt
any of my tables lasted a season

before a raging Argive brought an axe to it.
And fair enough. How much wibble-wobbling
can a man take before he loses his mind?

"This table here is my greatest achievement.
Look at the fine lines, marvel at the smooth surface.　　　　80
It was my family table, where we ate.
I had a wife and two children. My wife
worked not far, in a kitchen. When I met her,
I was stupid in a way you might know.
It took me a few times to realize
that her bright eyes were bright only for me.
She was lovely and I was blessed. We were happy.
Now my table had two people on its sides.
We had two children, a boy then a girl.
The table was now full, a person on each side.　　　　90
But there was something wrong with my beloved boy.
His body grew but his mind did not. Always

he remained a child, with a child's good heart
but also a child's weak understanding.
He helped me as best he could in my shop,
which made me happy, since he was close by.
One day he was hit by a cart, no ill will,
just an accident, the will of the gods.
I've never returned to that street since that day.
Bones were broken. He never healed. He died. 100
Now the table had an empty side. Much
did we weep. Then one morning my wife was working
a lamb and she cut her finger, just a nick, but
Hades took hold of that nick and wouldn't let go.
She died with much moaning and suffering.
Now the table had two empty sides. At least
I still had my girl. But in time she grew
and her life called her elsewhere. She married
and moved away. I was happy for her.
But now the table had three empty sides." 110

Said Psoas, "I too miss my wife and children.
Not an hour goes by that I don't think of them,
not a day that I am happy in their absence.
My heart has gone dark for not seeing them."

Asked Elanthius, "Then why have you come here?"

Said the son of nobody, "To win loot for them."

"And how much loot do you have so far, man?"

"Psoas is my name. None. Everything I've won
I've had to trade to stay alive. I have nothing."

Said Elanthius, "Then take my table, Psoas.   120
Bring it home. How many children do you have?"

Replied Psoas, "Two. A boy and a girl, like you."

"Then this is the perfect table for you."

Said Psoas, "It is indeed a fine piece of work.
Now go, run. Or hide. I will let you try your luck."

Replied Elanthius, "No, better to die rich
than to live bereft. The table is yours,
only make my passage to Hades quick."

The old man hardly grimaced as Psoas killed him.
The son of nobody surveyed the table.   130
It was too big. He could not carry it,
not in the chaos of battle. He moved on,
leaving behind a table with four empty sides.

The battle for the lower town (1–28): This is the second mention of Troy's lower town (see *The Arrival: The Good Country, the Walls of Troy*, page 75, line 110), and it is rich in details, accounting for what is barely mentioned in Homer: what the Greeks did for ten long years before the precipitous end of the war brought on by the trickery of the Trojan Horse. Not just a fretful siege, then, years of waiting around before an insurmountable wall, but, in addition, endless months of bloody urban warfare, house by house, street by street, in a conurbation that was vast and unfamiliar. No wonder the Greeks went crazy.

The wreckage at Troy was truly epic. The Greeks vengefully destroyed, subsequent peoples alternately rebuilt and pillaged for centuries and millennia, then time, through the agency of weather and vegetation, obliterated every other trace of Troy, until its legendary walls soared only in myth, like the Tower of Babel.

"I am a carpenter from Phrygia, but Troy has been my home for many years" (38–39): Speaking of Babel: a Phrygian living among Trojans talking to a Greek. The topic of translation should be addressed. *The Psoad*, like *The Iliad* and *The Odyssey*, was composed in the dactylic hexameter, the typical background thrum of classical Greek epic poetry, so six feet—the hexameter—of dactyls (often rounded out by a spondee or two). A Greek dactyl, to remind the interested reader, is a foot consisting of one long syllable followed by two short ones.

The word "harmony" is a dactyl in English, for example, HAR-mo-nee, TUM-ti-ti. (A spondee is made up of two long syllables.) The dactylic hexameter works very well in Ancient Greek. It flows. It doesn't flow in English; it's too long and dampens the crackling peppiness of the language. The iambic pentameter suited some English poets, Shakespeare, Milton, and so on, so five feet of iambs, the iamb being a foot of a short syllable followed by a long syllable, ti-TUM ti-TUM ti-TUM ti-TUM ti-TUM, like a heartbeat. But wanting your TUM-ti-tis to sound like ti-TUMs is like asking to have your shot of ouzo taste like Earl Grey.

And that's vintage songplay, anyway. Today is today, for today. Free verse is the new verse, has been for the last hundred years. In the tussle between fidelity to language and fidelity to meaning—so hard to get both—I have chosen the second. My concern has been purely to access and discuss content, the *what* of *The Psoad* rather than the *how*. I am neither George Chapman nor Alexander Pope, neither Robert Fagles nor Emily Wilson. So my translation feet wear neither dactylic nor iambic dance shoes, and the boom-box beat is neither the hexameter nor the pentameter. What you have here is an unfettered, barefoot attempt at a Greek folk dance, like Alan Bates trying to keep up with Zorba the Greek in the movie.

"We were happy" (87): Oh, so! Love is a purpose, a plan, an execution. Love is loud, love is quiet, a two-person symphony orchestra. Love is taking two

unfinished puzzles, pouring the remaining pieces into the same box, and completing a single picture. Love is picking a sofa. Love is having the same address. Love is two toothbrushes standing side by side. Love is choosing a baby's name. Love is alchemical, the great transmogrifier.

I loved Gail like a scribe loves a bard, like a candle loves a flame, like history loves the past, like a tongue loves speech, like a baby loves a honey-dipped finger.

"But there was something wrong with my beloved boy" (91): Once, in the depths of the biting English winter, when I was missing you terribly, I had a strange encounter with the fearsome Franklin Cubitt. I had come out of the Ancient World Library and it was dark. I turned the corner and right away I saw someone sitting on the sidewalk. I figured it was a drunk student, but it was him, Cubitt. He'd fallen and skinned his nose. It was bleeding. I was shocked.

"You've hurt yourself!" I cried.

It took him a few seconds to recognize me. I found his cane and helped him get up. I was dabbing his nose with a tissue when he said, "Today is the anniversary of my son's death."

"I'm sorry to hear that," I said.

"He had Down's syndrome. He essentially died of old age. How absurd, to outlive the dotage of your own son."

"It must have been very hard. What was his name?"
"His name was Rupert."
I didn't dare ask about any other children or a wife, in case there were none. I offered to walk him home and we walked a little ways.
"Do you have any children, Mr. Harlow?"
"Yes, I have a daughter."
"How old is she?"
"She's eight."
"Is she here with you at Oxford?"
"No, she's in Canada."
"Then what are you doing here? Go home, man, go home."
He waved me off and walked into the night, his cane going *tap, tap, tap*.

"*But there was something wrong with my beloved boy*" (91): Daddy I'm sick. Yuck.
That was it. A text from you on Mommy's phone. Four words. By the time I saw it, it was late for you and you would have been asleep, so I texted back: Sorry to hear. Have you been using your inhaler? Hope you feel better soon. Love you.

The Destruction of the Hinterland

We turned our attention to Troy's vassal cities:
Lyrnessus, Pedasus, all of Dardania,
Cilla, Pitya, and Hierapolis,
Percote, Sestus, and lovely Zelea,
Miletus, Arisbe and Practius,
Amydon, Larissa and fair Abydos,
Thebe Hypoplakia, and many others,
all cities that lived in the light of Troy.
Each one we razed to the ground, killing any
who resisted and all who were useless. 10
We took all livestock and every stockpile of grain,
anything of any worth, treasure or not,
gold and silver, fine leather and worked wood, of course,

but also fabric, furniture, and kitchenware,
anything that might make a man's hard life
before the walls of Troy more comfortable.
The kings got the best, leaving us the rest.

We razed the island of Tenedos, no one spared,
so that its rich waters could now be ours.
We attacked Mount Ida, whose green pastures   20
nourished the Troad. Their herds became ours.

But no matter how much of Troy we destroyed,
columns of Trojan confederates marched in
from far and wide, bringing men, arms, and provisions.
They came from great Hatti and mighty Persia,
from Canaan and Mesopotamia,
from as far as Aegypt and Aethiopia.
We saw that the world was a Trojan arsenal.

"all cities that lived in the light of Troy" (8): When the libraries of Oxford failed me, I turned to the benevolent, ever-giving octopus of interlibrary loans, or I sat in front of a computer screen, searching the digital journals and databases of countless institutions, luring this story out of oblivion. Thus did papyrus, parchment, paper, and even the Neo-Hittite cuneiform tablets of Boghazköi reveal to me the mysteries of *The Psoad*. But there comes a time when a story must be seen with one's eyes, felt in one's gut. History is geography. In pursuit of *The Psoad*, taking advantage of Europe's short distances and cheap flights, Franklin Cubitt be damned, I visited Athens, and Nafplio, the charming seaside town near the Mycenaean ruins of the northeastern Peloponnese, and Çanakkale, the buzzing Turkish city just north of the ruins of Troy at Hisarlik, jaunts of breathless excitement where sunlight, worn stone, sea breeze, and lapping waters brought Psoas directly to me. These are dots on a Psoadic map I will never forget. If I couldn't be with someone—you!—then I might as well be in a story.

"They came from great Hatti and mighty Persia, from Canaan and Mesopotamia, from as far as Aegypt and Aethiopia" (25–27): It is interesting to note the Eastern slant to Troy's sphere of influence, rooted in trade but flourishing

beyond the transactional nature of commerce into real loyalty. Among those hearing of Troy's grave travails would have been the varied inhabitants of Palestine, including Jews. Did Trojan and Jewish traders walk the streets of each other's great cities, Troy and Jerusalem, marvelling at their respective splendours? Were any Jewish guests entertained by the songs of peripatetic bards?

Lice, Fleas, and the Heart

At times the Trojans, their cymbals madly clanging
atop their walls, their trumpets blaring too,
chilling our hearts, poured out of their city
and marched on us, feet stomping, throats yelling,
in formations as broad as the horizon.

At other times, at dawn, at dusk, at night,
cymbals quiet, one formation behind the next,
they slipped out of their city without a sound
and rushed upon us, as quick as an arrow.

And always lice and fleas were upon us,   10
always the heart lay undressed and unprotected.
Many a spent man, alone in his tent,

face pressed to his sheepskin cover, wept bitterly.
I myself, by chance one night standing near his tent,
heard the son of nobody's muffled sobs.
What is one to do with the sadness of mortals?

"always the heart lay undressed and unprotected" (11): You don't get this in Homer, quite, this representation of war as a bleak, hopeless enterprise. In *The Psoad*, these notes of despair come repeatedly. Not for the likes of Psoas is the redemption accorded to Homeric heroes, who, because they have earned *kleos* and *timē*, glory and honour, will be remembered, and therefore, in a fashion, live on.

"What is one to do with the sadness of mortals?" (16): Can one really spend over two months not speaking to one's wife? Seemingly so. Every time I called now, either Gail did not answer, or you did. And if Gail's phone ever rang, it was always you. My wife only existed in terse emails.

The cost of airfare, her work, your school schedule—somehow it just didn't work out that you two could come to England for Christmas. I mailed cards and gifts to you and Gail, received a card and a gift from you. The festive season came and went, a lonely affair, if good for work. I missed you, I missed you terribly. Have I said that already? It's a gutting feeling to sense that others are doing fine without you, just fine.

Prince Mestor and the Son of Nobody Meet for the Second Time

"What? There, take that! And you—*this!* You're next, dog!"
Thus did Prince Mestor speak as he cut down
Argive after Argive, standing men reduced
by his mighty blows to the prostrate dead.
Those foes who thought to fight died facing him,
while those who turned to flee died with their backs to him.
His charge ended only when he chose to end it,
at the end of a long row of fallen men.
In his wake, the wild bedlam of battle stopped.
As water flees before a rock thrown into it,   10
just so fearful Argives fled the assault,
leaving the Trojans with no one to fight.

Soon war would start again, but for a moment
all men watched as Mestor's busy attendants,
following close, threshed the freshly harvested crop,
throwing anything good behind their line,
leaving naked Argive bodies in the dirt.
One man watching was Psoas of Midea,
who was killing the man he was fighting
just as Mestor's noisy onslaught went by them— 20
look! his sword is still in Tarkos of Zelea.
The son of nobody had stood his ground,
like a submerged rock around which water ripples.
Prince Mestor noted the one dead Trojan
in the line of Argives he had just killed.
Each man saw the other, and their gazes locked.

Said the high-born to the low-born, "Is that Tarkos?"

Replied the son of nobody, "It was."

With his sword, Psoas picked off the helmet
of the Zelean—it was quality— 30
and moved away, as battles started up again.
Much did he dwell on the unpleasant words
Prince Mestor of Troy had uttered to him.

"*killing the man he was fighting*" (19): [*ring*]
[*ring*]
[*ring*]
[*ring*]
[*ring*]
No answer.

"***Said the high-born to the low-born, 'Is that Tarkos?'***" (27): "Ah, is that you, Mr. Harlow? You have stooped to come to our weekly meeting and fulfill your academic duties. The citizens of Oxyrhynchus rise up and sing 'Hurrah, hurrah!'"

I began to tire of Professor Cubitt's grand Gothic office, all history, no life.

The Role of Horses

As you'll well know, Troy was famed for its horses,
and we'd looked forward to capturing their steeds.
But right away we noticed, astonished:
on the battlefield the Trojans went without them.
If a man was injured, it was no chariot
that brought him to safety, as was the custom
with our heroes, it was a tower shield,
flipped over, the man laid in the curve of it
and swiftly carried away by four comrades.
The trick did not deplete their forward line,   10
as usually it was men further back
who came to the rescue of the beleaguered man
and brought him to a safe spot away from the fight,
where a healer would tend to him right away.

We laughed at them, at first, at the Trojan men
who were carried off like produce from the field.
We were proud and we stuck to our ways and wheels.

But unhappily. One of our chariots
would near a fray to serve one of our heroes,
only for the horse to shriek as it was struck   20
by a spear or arrow, deliberately cast.

Yes, they who loved horses did the unspeakable:
they killed a steed rather than kill a man.

Soon this was a war fought with no horses—
don't let any other bard tell you otherwise.
Kings and commoners, we all walked into battle,
though it pleased the angry kings not at all.

To spite us, on feast days, the Trojans displayed

---

their most beautiful horses atop their walls.
We on foot, who walked to and from battle, 30
watched as a parade of radiant steeds
circled the sacred walls of Ilios.

Horse meat freshly roasted on a fire tastes good.
The son of nobody stayed strong on horse meat,
which he shared with me when he could find it,
until there was no horse meat to be found.

"Soon this was a war fought with no horses—don't let any other bard tell you otherwise" (24–25): This sure sounds like bardic rivalry, one tradition jostling with another. Might this explain why Homer never mentions Midea in *The Iliad*, to slight a tradition that claimed the city?

Given the comparative absence in *The Iliad* of vivid action involving the horse-and-chariot combo (other than when Achilles outrages Hector's dead body by dragging it behind his chariot around the walls of Troy near the end of Homer's epic), one would think a rival bard would grab the reins, so to speak, and deliver a precursor of the thrilling car chases of movies that never cease to entertain. But that is not the case. After this scene, horses and chariots vanish from *The Psoad*. It becomes, in a literal sense, a pedestrian epic.

What is the explanation for this curious feature of *The Psoad*, an epic that so abounds with animals, that it is anti-equine?

The Wealth of Troy

To strip the body of a Trojan fighter
was to bear witness to a recent bath.
Gleaming armour lined with thick soft white linen,
clean clothes that smelled of flowers, oiled hair that was cut,
a beard that was trimmed, finger and toe nails
that were clear and round—not a smirch anywhere
but for blood, while we were pigs in the mud,
we were pigs, we were pigs, we were pigs, grunting
as we stripped the man's sweet-smelling body, grunting
at the oil-rubbed smoothness of his skin, grunting   10
as we grew richer in lice, fleas, and rags.

"we were pigs in the mud, we were pigs, we were pigs, we were pigs" (7–8): This fragment strikes a surprisingly self-aware note. Whatever veracity might attend the Trojan War, we know that some few years after its storied end, Mycenaean Greece collapsed, the whole civilization, into the Greek Dark Ages. A debilitating war was no doubt one of the major factors behind this collapse. The Greeks were told they had won the war, but what victory was this? A generation of sons dead. Untold resources drained and wasted, with no treasure or land gained in return. The present times so hard and terribly uncertain. And all for what? The return of a man's wife. One wonders how a harried audience trying to make sense of this victory—a textbook Pyrrhic victory before the term was coined—desperate for good news, or, at the very least, an ennobling lesson, would take to being told four times over, "we were pigs". You've got to massage the message. That's certainly what the Homeric team was doing—it told aplenty of lost Greek lives, but every dead Greek boy was a hero, so handsome and valorous, just a little bit unlucky. Take Achilles. Hector kills his beloved friend Patroclus, yet still Achilles returns Hector's body to the Trojan's father, King Priam. Such a noble spirit. That is who we are, we Greeks, always the best even when we're the worse for it.

Perhaps this was the problem with the Psoadic bard: he was too stupidly honest to be sanctioned by posterity. Hopelessness is not a good tale. You need some sort of redemption.

"as we grew richer in lice, fleas, and rags" (11): Then it started to go wrong, one season at a time, one moment of weariness at a time. Aphrodite summoned Gail and me to our bedchamber, but that never ended the Trojan War. The goddess of love failed us—or, to put it in modern terms, taking on our agency, we failed her. Wit became sharpness. Contrast caused conflict. Habit turned to humdrum, while the unexpected led to turmoil. Caresses hid abrasions. I tired of Gail's practicality; there's more to life than the world before our eyes. She tired of my impracticality; there's more to life than the words coming out of our mouths. Erosion, fatigue, and disenchantment ground us down. Of course I got it wrong and made mistakes. An unkind word. A moment of slothfulness. A minor untruth. A sullenness. A withdrawal. Nothing ever dramatic, only chronic.

But this is no matter for Greek epic.

Achilles Kills Three Men

Fleet-footed Achilles, our great hero, charged
Mélotor of Thrakis, son of Dormon,
who was eager for the fight (fool fool fool),
and punched a spear into his chest with such force
that it went through him, lifting him off the ground.
Without pause, Achilles ran on and struck Oltos,
a Halizonian mason, in the side
as he was turning away, lancing him
clear across the torso, before he caught up with
Epístros the Carian, son of Evenus,					10
who hoped to flee, but instead was impaled
by Achilles with his long spear back to front,
making the man jump and all his limbs jerk
in uncontrollable dance. Three Trojans now

---

were transfixed upon the eleven-cubit spear,
each having let out a heart-stilling scream.
The god-blooded Argive, proud son of Peleus,
planted his spear upright into the ground,
so that there, in dripping blood, stood a sculpture
of man in his three warring emotions: 20
uppermost, the man who is hungry for war,
lying on his back, gazing at the blue sky
(his weeping mother); next, in the middle,
the man who hesitates and thinks better,
resting on his side, observing the life-giving,
blood-soaked earth (his weeping mother); and last,
the man who is full of fear and regret,
stretched face-down in the mud (his weeping mother).
Achilles did not pause to consider his work.
Instead, the next moment, he sheared the men off   30
with his sword, grabbed the bloody spear and threw it,
and down the field another man was dead,

standing next to Psoas, Nalnus, son of Proctet,
a weaver from Pontus, who didn't even see
who killed him. Next, Achilles, with his sword
studded with gems, chased down other terrified foes,
whom he cut down one after the other.

"grabbed the bloody spear and threw it" (31): Here is a perfect example of bardic confusion. There is a carefree indifference in the Trojan War traditions to the difference between a spear that is thrust, a pike, long and solid, and a spear that is thrown, a javelin, short and lithe, even though they are different and they would have been used, and carried, at different times. In this fragment, Achilles holds an "eleven-cubit spear" (15). The cubit was an ancient measure of length roughly equal to eighteen inches or forty-six centimetres, which means a spear 16.5 feet or 5.03 metres long. A pike. This is no doubt what Achilles was carrying into combat when he impaled Mélotor, Oltos, and Epístros. But after gruesomely "shearing" his victims off, would he realistically have picked off Nalnus "down the field" (32) with this same heavy device? It seems the bards instantly supply their warriors with whatever weapons they need in the moment, like in a video game.

This is yet another reminder of how, from hazy details, sharp bardic truth can still spring. Because war is still war, perhaps less artful, less effective, less heroic than the bards sing it, but still deadly, still widow-making and orphan-fathering, still tragic. On the canvas of the Trojan War, it is the depth of the colour that counts, not the exactitude of the lines.

The Death of Nastes

Nastes went into battle bedecked in gold
and coloured ribbons, as beautiful as a girl.
But his fair appearance did not save him from death,
since Achilles, there by the Símoïs,
brutally slew him and grabbed his finery,
leaving Psoas to find a ribbon or two.

"*Achilles, there by the Símoïs, brutally slew him*" (4–5): [*ring*]
[*ring*]
[*ring*]
[*ring*]
[*ring*]
Still no answer. How long could this last? Was it blindness or hope—or are they the same thing—that I didn't see that my phone rang in a heart's empty room?

"*leaving Psoas to find a ribbon or two*" (6): This short scene, nearly inconsequential, just the death of another man at the hands of Achilles, stands out because it appears in *The Iliad* in nearly the same terms. At the end of Book 2, Homer has it this way:

> And Nastes went into battle decked out in gold
> like a girl—fool that he was. But the gold could not save him
> from wretched death, when Achilles, there in the river,
> killed him, stripped him, and carried his gold away. (2.872–875)

As far as I can tell, this is the only place where the Homeric and Psoadic traditions directly intersect, as if on that day, by chance, both bards were there, both saw glittering Nastes die, and while Homer moved on, the other bard lingered, noting which river, and observing Psoas collect a coloured ribbon or two. In one version, Nastes dies by the river, in the other, *in* it, a small but eye-catching difference. Did the poor man stagger by the water's edge as Achilles was killing him?

    I wonder what Psoas did with the ribbons.

How Men Die

A man is injured. He cries, falls over.
He pants, his limbs and lips tremble, he is confused.
He takes note of the flight of his soul, he feels it,
that soft flight, and his staring eyes mirror it,
a terrified understanding, and then he's gone.

A spear hits Tenor's chest, making a slapping sound,
like a fish smacked against a rock to still it.
The look on the man's face, pure amazement,
like a small child seeing the sea for the first time.

Better off is he than the one who limps away,   10
because why do slowly what can be done quickly,
if it's unpleasant? An injured man cannot walk,

then cannot talk. The healer cannot wait.
Then the man cannot live. Healers are useless,
all of them, with their stinking poultices,
even Macháon, most famous of healers.
Why die at the hands of one pulling out
an arrow, when you can die at the hands
of the one who put it there in the first place?
Better at your fated hour, on time,   20
with the gods in battle, in glory, than
late in the company of useless men.

How a man dying madly loves the earth!
"O goddess Demeter!" gasps Photios,
"You are forever the life-giver, feeding
grapes, grains, and every other green creation,
so have mercy, please give me back my life."
But Demeter whispers, "Photios, harvest time
has come for you. I must feed you now to

grapes, grains, and every other green creation." 30

By blade or by point, there are many places
on a man's body from which life can slip away.
Man is a set of doors that will not stay latched.
Weeping Halnis, son of Myrdon, bleeds from his side
and goes grey, he who once was a chameleon.

How Men Die (title): [*ring*]
[*ring*]
A video call.
I answered, a smile upon my face. "Hello, Helen!"
It was Gail. I was astonished to see her.
"Hey. It's me. Helen is sick."
"Yeah, I know. She texted me. What's wrong?"
"Fever, cough, she's sore. She's staying home today."
"Of course. I'm sorry to hear she's not well."
"Not the best day for it. I've got a really important meeting. But I'll make it work."
"That must be stressful. Can I talk to her?"
"Let me see if she's awake."

You were asleep. It was nice to see your little face. I guess your mother was worried. Why would she have called otherwise, after so long? But it was strange. You were quite hardy, just a little asthma, and kids get sick all the time. Were you an excuse? Gail ended the call quickly. Did she regret her impulse? I gazed at my phone's screen, now dark, actively remembering our brief interaction, Gail's distinctive voice, the motions of her face, the dart and stare of her eyes.

Where is Psoas? (**passim**): Some may wonder how I determined that these Oxyrhynchus snippets belonged to *The Psoad*. There is no mention of Psoas, nor even of the Trojan War. But there is, first off, the mention of Demeter (24, 28). The appearance of a goddess barely mentioned by Homer already puts them in the orbit of *The Psoad*.

Furthermore, a line in a later fragment that is most certainly Psoadic has the following line:

> . . . the disbelief in their minds
> when the fated happens is like the look
> of a child the first time it sees the sea. (page 279, lines 21–23)

How similar to the look on Tenor's face (8–9), and further proof that this fragment belongs to *The Psoad*, snapping into place.

Most convincingly, there is the figure of speech concerning dying Halnis, who "goes grey, he who once was a chameleon" (35). Who but our Psoadic bard, fascinated by odd animals, would sing of a chameleon? And this is the second reference to a chameleon (see *The Arrival: The Good Country, the Walls of Troy*, page 77, line 149). The reptile is an Old World creature known since antiquity and found in Africa, Asia, and even, indeed, in southern Europe.

And speaking of odd animals (you'll like this one, Helen) . . .

The Trojans Bring in Entertainment

Out they came, long trains of burdened horses,
their bags bursting with riches of all kinds,
vessels of every prized metal, dazzling,
jewelry of the most precious stones, sparkling,
fine ceramics and pottery, exquisite,
wrought ivory and worked wood, sumptuous,
woven wool, linen, embroidered cloaks, beautiful,
all produced in Troy's endlessly fecund workshops,
now carried away before our staring eyes,
with rags of fresh colts jouncing along in tow.   10

What left a cocoon returned a butterfly.
Colts at the rear were now stallions at the front,
with a commander riding atop each,

and columns of armed men marching behind them,
while pack horses hauled every raw material,
even firewood gathered along the way.

One time they brought in the strangest creatures,
cream coloured with large brown spots, like leopards,
but nothing like leopards because taller
than any animal we had ever seen,   20
with long legs and longer necks, walking trees.
Understand me: we were in full battle,
Argive killing Trojan, Trojan killing Argive,
when these monsters silently stepped into view.
We, facing sacred Ilios, saw them first,
and·the amazement in our eyes made our foes turn,
so that they saw them, too. That amazement
spared many a life, as man after man,
even the heroes, chose to gawk rather than fight.
What creatures were these, conceived by what god?   30

Before the eyes of fifty thousand dumbstruck men,
they sailed into plain sight, as quiet as ships,
with a gait short, dainty, and undulating.
Astride each was a tiny man, a dwarf,
whose small size lent the creatures even more height.
These riders, gaily attired, waved at us
as they clung to the sloped backs of their beasts,
and some of us fighters, now children, waved back.

A Trojan trumpet blared and our foes retreated,
bubbling with good cheer. The Ilian Gate,   40
facing the plain, swung open in sight of all.
Standing there, arms as wide open as the gate,
was god-like King Priam himself, smiling broadly,
welcoming the creatures and their riders.
He was not alone. Around him, a seething throng,
were hundreds of children. Their full-throated delight
upon catching sight of the king's surprise,

such pure joy, reached our ears and pierced our hearts.
As the animals lumbered in, the dwarves climbed down
and started to dance to the sound of merry tunes. 50

We returned to our frayed tents and meagre meals.
The Trojans chose not to fight for a whole month.
Day and night, music, song, and laughter spilled over
their great walls, reaching our ears and piercing our hearts.
Many a spent Argive, alone in his tent,
face pressed to his sheepskin cover, wept bitterly.
I myself, by chance one night standing near his tent,
heard the son of nobody's muffled sobs.
What is one to do with the sadness of mortals?

"while pack horses hauled every raw material" (15): We can deduce from this fragment that the Trojans, while fighting for their lives, carried on with their manufacturing and trading, turning raw materials into valued goods, thus sustaining themselves during the lengthy war. One wonders how the Greeks kept afloat. The bard mentions the extensive pillaging of the Troad by the Greek forces (see *The Destruction of the Hinterland*, pages 120–21). Such stealing was certainly profitable, but not sustainable, hence the creeping pauperization of the Greeks at Troy, which comes through in a number of the fragments.

"with long legs and longer necks, walking trees" (21): These giraffes are presumably from Ethiopia, with whom the Ancient Greeks had imaginary and perhaps real relations. Not in Homer but in the *Aethiopis*, the now lost epic that followed *The Iliad* in the Epic Cycle, King Memnon of Ethiopia plays an important role. Needless to say, this fragment is unique to the Psoadic tradition. The creatures' appearance here is anonymous, which is curious. One would think that being seen, they would then be named. That's the usual order: eyes see, tongues stir. As a language, Ancient Greek was remarkably open to meeting and naming animals that existed beyond the small, dry peninsula where the Greeks originated. They saw and named the octopus, the dolphin, and the

medusa (jellyfish)—fair enough, they exist just out there, in the waters around Greece—but also, more remotely, the hippocampus (seahorse), the hippopotamus, and the elephant. All these words came to English from Ancient Greek. But the word for "giraffe" in Greek, καμηλοπάρδαλη, *kamilopárdali*, doesn't appear in Greek texts until the first century BCE. Are there strange bones waiting to be found in the ancient layers of Troy?

We have a bard who once again indulges in wilful animal exoticism. An intriguing possibility suggests itself: perhaps the animal exoticism of the Psoadic tradition pushed the Greek language toward new zoological horizons, the quirk of a single tradition of bards becoming the quirk of a language. If this is the case, it speaks of the authority *The Psoad* once enjoyed, that it could not only entertain the Greeks but expand the way they spoke.

The abundant presence of animals might also have a bearing on the epic's survival in Oxyrhynchus. The Egyptians practiced animal worship. Some gods had animal features: Anubis, for example, who had the head of a jackal, or

Khnum, who had the head of a ram. Or Thoth, the god of writing, who had the head of an ibis bird and was also closely associated with baboons. Cats and dogs were venerated. And so on, across Egypt, humans and animals living in an imaginary symbiosis. Perhaps the animal element in *The Psoad* appealed to the local sensibility.

"*Their full-throated delight upon catching sight of the king's surprise, such pure joy, reached our ears and pierced our hearts*" (46–48): Ancient Greek epic is usually thought of as adult entertainment, but I wonder if these animals were not thrown in to entertain younger listeners.

"*Many a spent Argive, alone in his tent, face pressed to his sheepskin cover, wept bitterly*" (55–56): I wept and wept and wept.

The Complaint of Thersites

"Son of Atreus, what's your new complaint?
Are you short on gold? Feel cramped in your tent
by all the plunder we have given you?
Need a few more beautiful women, captured
at our risk, to serve you in and out of bed?
Or was your roast lamb undercooked last night?
What more do you want of us, we who have gained
nothing from this war but pain, loss, and grief?"

Said this and more Thersites to Agamemnon
in front of all the men, at times scolding, 10
at times mocking the red-faced King of Kings
over the conduct of the war. He was cut short.
King Odysseus strode up and thrashed him.

His staff fell on Thersites many times over,
with a thud when hitting flesh (how he yelped!),
with a crack when hitting bone (how he cried!).
All his teeth he spat out, like olive pits,
having much the same colour and texture,
such was the force of the King of Ithaca's blows
(and the quality of Thersites' teeth).   20
His battered face turned to a berry-jam pot
that has fallen onto stone from a high shelf.
Purple welts swelled all over his body. Ribs cracked.
It was a wonder the staff didn't break
(or more bones). Thersites escaped the king's wrath
on all fours, crawling to his tent, where he collapsed
and did not stir for the rest of the day.
The welts on his body oozed blood and pus.
He groaned and writhed in pain and cried out from thirst,
but no one among the Argives came to him,   30
until brotherly love rose in Psoas,

who made his way through and out the Argive camp
to Thersites' bedraggled tent on the hill.

Along the way, Adrephonous of Corinth,
a rugged fighter who never shirked from battle,
saw the son of nobody and cried out to him,
"Stop, Psoas. It looks to me like you're going to see
that man most reviled by our fearless kings."

Replied Psoas, "If you mean Prince Paris,
no I'm not. I am going to see our friend Thersites. 40
But tell me, Adrephonous, was it not he
who just the other day risked his life to save yours?
I saw it. I was there. You were sword fighting,
blade and shield clashing against your Trojan foe's,
when a flung rock hit your helmet, knocking it off—
you were stunned, staggered, would have died, an easy kill,
if Thersites had not seen your trouble,

shield-shoved aside his own foe and lunged for yours,
stabbing him where he hoped to stab you, in the neck,
right through, before turning back to his own fight. 50
Is that not how it went, Adrephonous?"

Adrephonous did not reply but walked off,
and Psoas walked on. But along the way,
Elatiön of Pylos, a healer,
saw the son of nobody and said to him,
"Stop, Psoas. It looks to me like you're going to see
that man most reviled by our fearless kings."

Replied Psoas, "If you mean Prince Hector,
no I'm not. I am going to see our friend Thersites.
But tell me, Elatiön, was it not he 60
who just the other day rallied some men
so that they might gather various roots and herbs
for your poultices? I saw it. I was there.

In a line, under his watchful eye, we searched
the land until sunset, after battling all day.
Is that not how it went, Elatiön?"

Elatiön did not reply but walked off,
and Psoas walked on. But along the way,
Hypéradas of Mycenae, a priest,
saw the son of nobody and whispered to him, 70
"Stop, Psoas. It looks to me like you're going to see
that man most reviled by our fearless kings."

Replied Psoas, "If you mean King Priam,
no I'm not. I'm going to see our friend Thersites.
But tell me, Hypéradas, was it not he
who just the other day helped you with the rites
to Apollo? I saw it. I was there.
It was not the showy, front-row work he did,
holding the animals before the god

as their throats are slit, or at the roasting, 80
when the god is appeased. No, it was the herding
done afar, away from your splendid robes and talk.
Is that not how it went, Hypéradas?"

Hypéradas did not reply but walked off,
and Psoas walked on to Thersites' tent.
He pushed aside the ragged flap, entered,
and sat down next to his aching comrade.
Said he to him, after giving him water,
"You're a stupid goat. That's not how to speak
to a king, least of all the King of Kings. 90
Do that again and it will be with his sword,
not his staff, that Odysseus beats you."

Thersites opened his swollen eyelids,
like slugs parting company, and replied he,
his voice quiet and raspy, "Why shouldn't I give

a piece of my mind to that upright pig?
Nine years we've been here, with no end in sight,
all because his moron of a brother
couldn't hold on to his wife. Tell me, Psoas,
would a shepherd who has a flock of one sheep   100
lose that one sheep to the wolves? Of course not.
But dumb Menelaus to a prancing wolf cub
managed to lose his single pretty ewe.
We're paying for that loss, over and again.
Look at my tent. It looks like it has mange.
My body aches from the hard ground I sleep on.
We're starved because our rations are loathsome.
In battle every day I must kill good men
who have done me no wrong, sons, husbands, fathers,
or die at the hands of good men I have not wronged.   110
What unbearable life is this for a man?
Why should I do it? Where is my reward?
Yet *I'm* a stupid goat, son of nobody?

Meanwhile, those kings, in their palatial tents
filled to the ceiling with loot and treasure,
spend their nights feasting on the best wine and food
and cavorting in orgies with beautiful girls
captured from cities we razed at our peril.
War is the dearly loved child of gods, kings, and bards.
Watch them, the fancy Argive kings of song,   120
as they laugh, dance, feast, and live forever,
while we die miserable, anonymous deaths.
Who will sing of me, who will sing of you?
Why are we so little deserving of song?
Yet *I'm* a stupid goat, son of nobody?"

Psoas heard, and replied he to Thersites,
"I gathered the teeth you lost—here they are.
A man likes to be buried with all his bones."
He tossed the teeth and they rolled on the ground like dice,
and the two men looked at them as they would dice,   130

musing on their fate. Would they win, would they lose?

The son of nobody cleansed Thersites' wounds,
brought him water and food, stayed with him in his tent,
watching over him for three days and three nights.
When Thersites managed to get to his feet,
Psoas helped him to the shore, where he washed and wept.
Said Thersites to the son of nobody,
"No one came to comfort me, none whom I helped,
none whom I saved. Only you came, with no want
or fear, only brotherly love. For this,   140
Psoas of Midea, I will thank you.
When we die and we come to drink from the river
that makes us forget, know that I will not drink
the drop that makes me forget you. And while I live,
I shall not forget you in some other way."

"Said this and more Thersites to Agamemnon" (9): Thersites is the only commoner to speak in *The Iliad*—and only one time—and his speech in Homer's epic is very similar to the one here, a rant against Agamemnon. Homer also has Thersites get roughed up by Odysseus, but with just one mighty wallop. His real abuse comes in his portrayal of the commoner:

> The ugliest man in the army that came to Troy,
> he was bowlegged and lame in one foot, and his shoulders hunched
> over his chest; his head was pointed; upon it
> sprouted a few sparse patches of scraggly hair. (2.216–219)

Such a picture can only be a caricature. It makes clear Thersites' low status. Yet in *The Iliad*, too, he speaks with conviction. And to our modern minds, his tirade against Agamemnon seems entirely justified. Why indeed should an ordinary man risk his life every day for ten years with minimal reward to satisfy the greed and lust of a pampered despot? Psoas answers none of Thersites' sharp, rhetorical questions, only sits in support of him. Yet the iniquities of their fate, nicely symbolized by the roll of Thersites' teeth-dice, resonates with him. How else to explain the fragments that follow, which are the key actions of the epic? Psoas would not do what he does if he had not fully heard his companion. Thersites' verbal rebellion is the prelude to Psoas's physical rebellion.

"the river that makes us forget" (142–143): The river Lethe, of forgetfulness, one of the five rivers of Hades.

"the river that makes us forget" (142–143): [*bzzz*]
[*bzzz*]
[*bzzz*]
[*bzzz*]
[*bzzz*]
I didn't reply. I'd left my phone in my bag, ringer off, notifications off. Those are the rules of the libraries at Oxford. I just didn't hear it. I was working and work was going well.

"And while I live, I shall not forget you in some other way" (144–145): There was a click in my mind when I came upon this line. A fascinating, unverifiable, but eminently plausible possibility suggested itself to me at that moment: Thersites was the original bard of *The Psoad*, the first to sing of the son of nobody. Hence the coarser language and imagery. Hence the hero celebrated, a commoner. Hence the last line in the *Prologue*: "he was my friend" (page 14, line 10). It was one son of nobody singing of another. From now on in my mind it was no longer "the Psoadic bard"; it was "Thersites the bard". Homer's scathing portrayal of him in *The Iliad* might now be seen as a sign of animosity between two bardic traditions.

In the *Aethiopis*, Thersites also makes an appearance, and as in *The Iliad*, it is not a happy one. Quintus of Smyrna, in his *The Fall of Troy*, expands on the episode. Achilles has just killed Penthesilea, Queen of the Amazons, an effective ally of the Trojans who has cost the Greek forces many lives. She lies dead on the battlefield, and Achilles, moved by her beauty ("a lovely face, lovely in death," says Quintus), falls in love with her. Thersites confirms his reputation as one whose truth-telling is personally unwise: he ridicules Achilles to his face. He says to the hero, in essence, *You love her, do you? Wished you'd made her your wife? Well, it's a bit late, mate—you just impaled her with your big spear. And she was our bitter enemy, need I remind you? I can't count how many of our men she killed. What's more important to you, your lust or your country?* Achilles does not react well to Thersites' insights, according to Quintus:

> A sudden buffet of his hand . . .
> Smote 'neath the railer's ear, and all his teeth
> Were dashed to the earth. He fell upon his face.
> Forth of his lips the blood in torrent gushed.
> Swift from his body fled the dastard soul . . .

The punch is so hard that it kills Thersites. As he did when he mocked

Agamemnon, Thersites rattles the cage of the social order, and, once more, he is brutally punished for it.

Curious, the mention of the loss of his teeth in Quintus. It's the same as in *The Psoad*. What's with Thersites' teeth? Perhaps an elite of bards, defenders of a narrative status quo, were asserting their dominance by getting rid of a troublesome rival—hence why they twice get his teeth knocked out, to silence his mouth, a bard's main instrument.

The Psoad now had an author, whence the tale came, its germ, its first soil. Henceforth, the name Thersites would sound different, no longer just a maligned character with a big mouth, but one with a "soaring cave" whose fluttering tongue would give "glory" (see *Prologue*, page 14, lines 6–7).

"And while I live, I shall not forget you in some other way" (144–145): "Daddy, tell me a story."

How many times did you ask me that, Helen? I have always been your storyteller, your bard. How about this one, about battles and boiling rage?

"Well, there he is."

Psoas saw him in the line of opposing men,
there, not far from the banks of the Scamander,
and shouted he to him, "Golon of Epicus,
is that you? It is, isn't it? I know it.
You don't spend ten years fighting your enemy
without getting to know him. We clash and retreat,
clash and retreat again, over and over,
and each time we come back with some small knowledge
of the man whose shield we struck with our sword,
who tried to get at us with a spear but missed.　　　　10
This knowledge is useful, is it not, Golon?
Of course, you could strike at a stranger foe.
That man there, for example, do you know him?
Yes, that one. You shake your head. I thought so.

His name is Lóracus and he hails from Phthia.
A Myrmidon, one of fierce Prince Achilles' men,
a bronzesmith by trade and good at dice, now you know—
and I know what you're thinking: *A bronzesmith,*
therefore strong of arms but not so of legs,
so perhaps a mighty hitter, but slow to turn. 20
And a lover of dice, so perhaps given
to foolish risk-taking, if challenged just right.
Such are your calculations, isn't that so?
Hence why, as we move forward in battle,
clanging our swords against our shields and glaring,
we seek a familiar enemy,
to avoid the stranger foe's unknown skills.
But you, Golon of Epicus, I know you.
I know only your mother wept when you left home,
since you no longer have a living father, 30
and she is alone in this cold, harsh world
where the gods care nothing for us mortals.

I know your wife, two boys and two girls also wept,
since they feared they would never see you again,
and they are right, they won't. And I say further
that you are a beekeeper and candlemaker,
the best in Epicus, the man people trusted
when they wanted to sweeten their food or wine,
or when the time came to push back the darkness,
but candles won't save you today, Golon,   40
from the darkness that is coming your way.
I know you are quick enough on your feet,
how you dodge and parry, like this, like that—but
you are not as quick as you'd like with your sword,
are you, Golon? You should mind your right side.
Still more, I know that on many a night
you sweetened the sleep of your baby girl
with a finger dipped in your golden honey
to the dancing flame of one of your candles.
And it is the same with you, is it not?   50

As you are pushed forward by the tide of battle,
you scan the enemy line, seeking a known foe.
Then you see me and your fear has a glad focus.
You shout, 'Psoas of Midea, is that you?'
I shout back with equally violent glee
and we rush at each other, elated.
I will kill you, Golon of Epicus,
so that as I strip your body I can say
with full knowledge, 'I killed Golon of Epicus.'
So come now, my abhorred friend, let us fight." 60

The two men threw themselves at each other,
and so it was that day: Psoas of Midea
with his sword killed Golon of Epicus
because the beekeeper did not mind his right side.
His baby girl would never again go to sleep
with his honey-dipped finger in her mouth
to the dancing flame of one of his candles.

Now sometimes the battle line was a forest,
still and fixed, each fighter a woodcutter.
But on this day, this day of which I sing,　　　　　　　　70
the battle was like a raging storm at sea.
Though each man thought he was captain of his ship,
the winds and the waters pushed him about
until he was overwhelmed and feared capsizing.
Why was the battle a raging storm this day?
Maybe it was because a great fighter,
a hero, had stepped onto the stage of war,
lion-raging Achilles or wolf-fierce Hector,
perhaps Diomédes or Sarpedon,
warriors who strode across the Trojan plain　　　　　　　　80
not like men but like gods scything a field,
twenty men falling at every swing of the scythe.
But they need not even move, these heroes.
They might very well appear and just *stand*,
stock-still, and the effect would be the same:

a deepening wave of terror that rippled out
across the entire battlefield until
even men who had seen nothing felt it.

Or it might be something random: two men who
by chance turned to retreat at the same time,   90
a fearful third who saw them and took fright
and passed on that fright to four other men,
and so a stampede starts, with no father
but a great number of running children.

So it happened this day of which I sing.
A disturbance rippled across the battlefield
until it came to the man who had just killed
Golon of Epicus, Psoas of Midea,
who was stripping his enemy's body.
Who knew a beekeeper at war would dress so well?   100
Such a fine taslet, such a soft tunic.

The son of nobody meant to take it all.
The dead man's body flopped this way and that
until he was naked from head to toe.
Then thick-bodied Psoas felt the wave, heard the wind.
He lifted his head. He hoped to hold his ground
as his loot still lay scattered around the body.
But from his left came an unstoppable wave.
The trample of feet. A swelling chorus of shouts.
The flash of raised swords. The arc of flying arrows. 110
A rock's near miss. A spear's perfect landing.
A man's startled expression. Another's glad yell.
Pushing, shoving. Falters, falls. A moving wall.
The wave was close, was nearly upon him.

As every man around him felt, so Psoas felt:
he must run—or be taken to Hades.
He turned and ran, like every man around him,
a mad dash over the stony Ilian plain,

colliding every which way into other men.
Some stumbled, some tripped, some fell to the ground.   120
Psoas raced in a blind, headlong panic,
carried along while he tried to push through.
He ran as fast as his legs would carry him
until the tide of men seemed to slacken.
He faltered to a stop and looked around, breathless.

Meriones, son of Molus, was next to him,
Crete's noble son, who always fought with the best,
champion at killing running men, groin-damager.
He noticed the son of nobody at his side.

Said Meriones, "What happened, why did we flee   130
with such terror? Was it Prince Hector himself?
How is it that his voice is always heard
above the din of war, though he never shouts
but only speaks, as if in conversation?

Like a cloaked spy, his voice slips through the ranks,
unnoticed, unstopped, until it reaches our ears.
Nothing arouses quaking fear like that man's lisp.
So, tell me, was it him?" But Psoas shook his head,
since he had neither seen nor heard Hector.

Said Meriones, "If Hector is around,   140
we can do nothing, so wolf-fierce is he,
so I will wait here, since I don't want to die.
Wait here with me, Psoas of Midea,
until we see what the gods want of us."

They stood, side by side, panting and watchful,
the son of Molus and the son of nobody.
But the gods are impatient in mortal matters
and soon the wind carried a voice to their ears.

"Brave men of Argos, what are you doing?

Shall we run all the way back to our homeland, 150
the Trojans nipping at our heels like dogs
chasing a flock of sheep back to their pen?
Is that the kind of men we are? No, I say!
Who will join me in pushing back the Trojans?"
It was the King of Argos, Diomédes,
a man who had never known fear in his life.
His strong voice and brave words were heard by all men.
The great wave had passed, the storm had died down.
Now the battlefield seemed like a forest
in which a man might sensibly place his courage. 160

Meriones and Psoas looked at each other.
Each now tightened the strap of his helmet,
one, with a horsehair crest, the other, without.
Each now set right his breastplate and backplate,
one, burnished bronze, the other, wood stitched on linen.
Each now made sure his sword slid with ease from its sheath,

one, gem-studded, trusty, the other, plain, rusty.
Each now inspected the spear in his hand,
one, with an ashen shaft, the iron point fixed
by a gold ring, the other, usable.   170
Each now leaned over and secured his greaves,
one, burnished bronze, the other, wood stitched on linen.
Each now went bent-kneed to adjust his sandals,
one pair, the straps and soles sturdy, the other, worn.
Each now looked over the face and straps of his shield,
one, of the best bronze and thickest oxhide,
inlaid with gold and silver, tough and sturdy,
the straps triple-stitched, the other, good enough.
They stood, one man as bright as gems, the other, brown.

Once they were ready, they took a deep breath   180
and moved together closer to the front line
where war was alive and men were dying.
They scanned the jostling wall of Trojan shields,

trying to make out the fighting man behind each,
seeking where they might advance, whom they might challenge.
Who would be fit for Lord Meriones,
what high-born son of Ilios might he fight?
What low-born might the low-born next to him fight?

Was it Lord Meriones, then, Crete's noble son,
who uttered the fateful words to Psoas— 190
or was it Lord Hades of the Underworld,
in the guise of Meriones, who said it?
But if it was Hades, why would the god do that?

Meriones, son of Molus, turned to Psoas,
and said he to him, "Tell me, yesterday
were you not the one looking for Prince Mestor,
one of the fifty sons of King Priam,
a killer of men whose mere gaze brings on trembling
in his foes, truly a bastion of sacred Troy?"

Lord Meriones pointed. "Well, there he is." 200

Psoas heard the words, and right away his heart jumped, his chest heaved, and he filled with boiling rage.

Psoas's speech to Golon (3–60): Any reader of *The Iliad* will notice how loquacious the Greeks and Trojans are in battle. They constantly talk not only to their comrades but to their opponents. It's as if they are neighbours chatting over a fence rather than enemies fighting on a battlefield. This is where and how Greek epic makes its commentary on reality. Upon an actual fight between two men, a bard superimposes analysis and insight, melding the two so that his audience gets both action and examination. This is augmented, interpreted history the same way the Gospels are augmented, interpreted biography.

Although, to be truthful, ancient battles were indeed more sociable affairs than modern wars. Consider the posture of the fighter. In Homer's and Psoas's war, the fighter, Greek or Trojan, stands bolt upright and goes about in plain sight, conversing with his friends and haranguing his enemies, scowling at them eye to eye. Compare this to modern wars—take your pick—where the stock image is of a soldier lying flat on the ground. This man, who has never actually seen his foe, if he has to get up, scurries bent over like a hunchback in a state of blank terror, hoping to throw himself down to the ground again as soon as he can. The fear of this horizontal soldier is justified: in an instant the air around him may be saturated with machine-gun or artillery fire, or he may be felled by a sniper. For Homer's vertical soldier, on the other hand, it seems a pair of sharp eyes and a good shield are enough to deal with the nuisance of spears and arrows. The modern warrior is fearful of his anonymous enemy's far-reaching technology. The Homeric and Psoadic warrior is fearful of his actual enemy.

But it's still a war that's on here, not a garden party. Soon enough, after all the long speeches have been delivered and heard, an arm will be severed, a skull will be shattered, a man's life will end.

"His baby girl would never again go to sleep with his honey-dipped finger in her mouth to the dancing flame of one of his candles" (65–67): [*bzzz*]
[*bzzz*]
[*bzzz*]
[*bzzz*]
[*bzzz*]
Gail called again two minutes later. Once again, I didn't hear the phone.

"Such a fine taslet" (101): A taslet is an armoured skirt of metal plates worn at the waist to protect the groin area.

"groin-damager" (128): Speaking of taslets. The locution is as odd in Ancient Greek (ὀλοός βουβῶνι, *oloós vouvóni*) as it is in English. Did Lord Meriones happen to injure a number of men in their groin area, and it came to the notice of others? If there is symbolism here, it's lost to time.

"Nothing arouses quaking fear like that man's lisp" **(137):** Homer makes no mention of any speech impediment on Hector's part, perhaps in deference to his status as a great hero. But in *History of the Fall of Troy*, by Dares the Phrygian, mentioned earlier, Hector is also described as having a lisp.

The two men getting ready **(162–179):** That so few bronze breastplates have been found in archaeological digs, despite their constant mention in Homer, hints that most men protected themselves with more perishable materials. Which seems about right. Neither copper nor tin, the base elements of bronze, is to be found on mainland Greece. Very likely, poor soldiers were poorly kitted out, protecting themselves with whatever common materials were at hand. The bard offers here a fascinating tidbit about one ordinary man's armour, an early version of a gambeson: "wood stitched on linen" (165, 172). It doesn't sound like a bad idea. Linen is quite a sturdy fabric, especially in multiple layers, while wood is easy to find, carve, and replace. Wood strips could be fitted to the shape and movements of the body, and would do a fair job of blunting the blow of a sword or reducing the impact of a spear or arrow.

But we have no proof of this contrivance beyond what is said here, words clinging to what is lost to time.

The Catalogue of Sons

There he stood behind enemy lines, Prince Mestor,
one of the fifty sons of King Priam,
a brother to all the princes of Troy,
Hector, Paris, Demócoön, Echémmon,
Chrómius, Gorgýthion, Isus, Ántiphus,
Dóryclus, Cebríones, Polydórus,
Lycáon, Troilus, Hélenus, Pammon,
Ágathon, Antíphonus, Polítes,
Deíphobus, Hippóthoüs, Dius,
Archion, Dólagus, Ascániöpes,   10
Arégoras, Polýmachus, Ástyachon,
Bíätas, Chérsias, Glaucónius,
Hypómedon, Telónius, Lysídocus,
Máchander, Ídagus, Prólius, Chroön,

Palísides, Herósacus, Brodámas,
Dólamon, Andrónachus, Erábias,
Clonon, Áltias, Antóldon, Lýcatus,
Íliacos, and Strómacon, each one
dearly loved by his father and mother,
who watched for them every day from the high walls, 20
recognizing each son without effort,
knowing not only their martial raiments
but the motions of each, his walk and his turns,
since the man moved much like the child once had,
the little wooden stick now a bronze sword.

The list of names (4–18): A list—whether of the names of war dead or of produce to be bought at the grocery store—can have a strange appeal. A list demands a more active attention of the mind, a willingness to participate in its purpose. A list yearns for wholeness, which mirrors a similar yearning in all of us—an incomplete list is not only unfulfilled but unfulfilling. A list, by virtue of its point-by-point construction, staccato, every element similar in status, equal, lends itself to a special sort of recitation, exalted, at the very least mindful. A list is memory's favourite difficult child.

And so here. This Catalogue of Sons could just be a tedious declamation of stillborn characters, a roller-coaster ride of tonic accents and diaereses, a delight to Greek anthroponymists but no one else. Perhaps it was nothing more than a pause before the plunge into the main action, a good time to skip out to the restroom. Maybe it was an opportunity for a bard to show mnemonic prowess. It could have been just a standard item in the Psoadic tradition, dull but required, at least mercifully shorter than Homer's endless Catalogue of Ships.

Or maybe this: these adored, once-living children were known to ancient audiences through stories now lost, and this recitation of their names, delivered slowly and mindfully, was actually deeply moving, not a catalogue, but a dirge. They all die, after all; that is the grimness of the tale, that a father and a mother must watch from their city walls as every one of their sons is killed (and their daughters who are spared reduced to domestic and sexual slavery). So perhaps this was one of those lists: special, revered.

The list of names (4–18): For Priam and Hecuba, fifty lost sons and a hundred lost daughters. For many ancient audiences, how many lost sons and daughters to war, to want, to disease?

The list of names (4–18): For me, just one precious daughter, just you, my Helen.

The list of names (4–18): What is one to do with the sadness of mortals?

Psoas Threatens Prince Mestor

Psoas recognized the prince in his splendid dress
and resplendent shield, and right away his heart jumped,
his chest heaved, and he filled with boiling rage.
Shouted the son of nobody to the Trojan prince,
"Lord Mestor, come closer so that I might kill you!"

Standing at a distance behind the front line,
the Trojan prince was not fighting at that moment
and seemed not to hear what the Midean had said.
Shouted the son of nobody to the Trojan prince,
"Mestor, I am no less of a man than you are. 10
Today I shall prove it, when by my hands you die!"

War stopped, as those who were fighting stopped
   their battling
and those who were resting stopped their talking.
There, not far from the banks of the Scamander,
across the line of opposing foes, men stared.
What impudence! The nerve of the man! Who is he?
Is he an idiot? A fool? Both? Who is he?
You must understand that heroes cut down
ordinary men like blades of grass are scythed,
and never did a blade of grass try to strike back.   20
What chance would a goat-teat puller, a cheesemaker,
a fixer of fences, a field lazer-about,
have against a man who knew fine metal,
both sharp and pointed, who knew every thrust
and every feint, who knew the history and practice
of warfare like a mother knows her child,
a highly trained highest-born, *a prince of Troy.*

Why would Hades do that? Why would he knock
against the sacred order of being,
as if a clod of earth could order a cloud   30
to come down from the sky and lie under its feet?
Why did Hades infect Psoas with such rage?

Perhaps it was the roll of Thersites' teeth-dice.
They rolled and they tumbled—how light dice are—
then revealed his losing fate, black on white.
Was this the augury that set Psoas on fire?
Is this how the cheesemaker got the mettle
to seek out a highest-born who knew metal?
Is this how the clod of earth found the nerve
to order a cloud to lie under its feet?   40
But if it was Hades, why would the god do that?
The gods know, but they always keep their secrets.

    Into the expectant silence, the prince called,

"What is that braying I hear? Is that Psnotnose,
the hunchback with the limp and the greasy face
covered in spots, scars, pimples and clogged pores?
With the big, sticking-out ears, the gummy mouth
with five black teeth, and the incessant facial tics?
With the too-long arms and the too-short legs?
Whose father was a slug in a lettuce? 50
Whose mother was a split-eyed chameleon?
Who brays like a donkey, annoys like a fly,
and smells like a ferret? I know that man,
can smell him now. He is the son of nobody.
I can't count how many times I've come close
to killing him, only to have him run away
on his bowed and stumpy legs, quaking with fear,
sprays of shit loudly blasting out of his arse.
Oh, the nightly laundry when you are a coward.
Yet I am no more of a man than he is." 60

Men, both Trojan and Argive, laughed at Mestor's words,
at how the prince could spin humour out of horror.
Around him arose a chorus of *pffft*, *pffft*, *pffft*,
as weary nobles had a mirthful moment.

Continued the prince, with menace in his voice,
"Know your place and quit your vain threats, Psoas.
You can attempt to take but do not mistake.
That which is mine is mine, always will be,
and mine is the love of my wife and children,
and mine is the love of my father and mother,   70
and mine is the honour of my sacred duty,
and mine is the righteousness of my cause,
and mine is the high regard in which I am held,
and mine is my imperishable lineage,
and mine is the very sharp blade of this sword.
Today, as when the farmer steps into the yard,
you will run like a chicken, wings flapping.

Yet I am no more of a man than you are."

Men, both Trojan and Argive, laughed at Mestor's words,
at how the prince could spin humour out of horror. 80
Around him arose a chorus of *squawk, squawk, squawk,*
as weary nobles had a mirthful moment.

Shouted Psoas, "Come, dark-haired purple man,
hero at words, dandy on the dance floor.
This day, believe me, you will eat those words!"

Mestor advanced to the line of stalled battle,
his eyes shifting left and right, left and right.
He lifted his visored helmet a little.
On his face was not a scowl but a wicked smile.

Said the prince to the son of nobody, 90
"Is that it? Is that your best, you fabulous bard?

A trite boast? I will eat my words, you say?
Tell me, these edible words, are they baked or boiled?
Are they commonly considered a meat dish?
Do they come with sauce? Can I put honey on them?
I weary of you, Psmallbrain. But speaking of food,
we watch what you Argives eat, and we wonder.
You clear the plain of rats and dogs, thank you—
but stork? Who eats stork? And really, *tortoises?*
Is this how men are made in Achaea? 100
We rather eat lamb and goat, beef and pork,
carved and cut into small pieces and skewered.
The embers of a fire are spread thinly
and the juicy spits are laid on a rack.
The meat is sprinkled with spices and holy salt,
roasted to perfection, then heaped on a platter
and served with fresh bread and cups of Pramnian wine
spiced with onions, grated goat's cheese, and white barley,
followed by oat cakes soaked in golden honey.

Oh, I can just smell it. Can you, Pslowfat? 110
And fires at night are bright and our eyes are keen,
so don't think we haven't noticed how low you stoop.
We see a stick with a skinny fish on it,
then the fish is gone and something more substantial
is put to roasting. The fat crackles in the fire,
sending up shoots of flame, and the lean shape
becomes clear. Do you think that just because
it's on a spit we don't recognize the shape
of a human arm, the fingers tightly curled?
Psoas,"—the prince snarled—"you're just a mangy dog!" 120

At that very moment, sent by Apollo,
who hated the Argives and loved the Trojans,
a sniffing dog appeared between the two men.
What was this animal doing, poking about
in broad daylight amidst men in pitched battle?
During the day, men held the stage alone.

It was at night that the creatures came out,
of every kind and size, scaled, feathered, and furred.
We tried to bury our dead with all proper rites,
but as the war dragged on, customs were abandoned   130
as we fell prey to deprivation and despair.
The bodies of countless men were abandoned
and at night the plain buzzed as countless creatures
worked their jaws on the sorry dead, while we,
the sleepless hollow-eyed living, tried to rest.
Fights erupted on occasion, with barks and shrieks,
but mostly it was a quiet, fervid meal.
When the Trojans clanged their cymbals from their walls,
which they did every dawn to disturb our sleep,
a vast carpet of foul eaters lifted off   140
from the field, revealing another layer
of foul eaters: rats, jackals, wolves, wild cats, bears,
and dogs, so many dogs. Dogs were everywhere.
They skulked about with the stealth of shadows—

shadows with teeth. Why cross a living man
when so many dead ones were on offer?
They were silent, watchful and timorous.
But this dog dared to appear now,
next to Prince Mestor and the son of nobody.
Mestor raised his sword and with a swift, clean blow   150
slew the cur in two, straight across the back.
At once, acted upon by Apollo,
the front half of the dog reared up its head and,
precariously balancing, staggered forward,
while the back half, tail tightly tucked between its legs,
did the same in the opposite direction.
The dog, now two two-legged creatures, tottered
a few steps on the battlefield, then fell over.

"See, *see!*" roared Mestor. "That is what you are!
A blind, laughable two-legged creature!   160
Yet I am no more of a man than you are."

Men, both Trojan and Argive, laughed at Mestor's words,
at how the prince could spin humour out of horror.
Around him arose a chorus of *arf, arf, arf,*
as weary nobles had a mirthful moment.

Said the prince to the son of nobody
in a voice that had the calm of a lake,
"Come then, shrub-man, come strike at the sun above you."

The prince raised his sword and moved forward two steps.
The son of nobody retreated a pace.   170
Would Psoas be true to his fighting words,
and would he now attack the Trojan prince?
Men watched, as the two fiercely stared at each other.

The prince took a hand and with one motion
raised his taslet and pulled aside his tunic,
exposing his prick, which flopped down and dangled.

Then he let go and with that same strong hand
took hold of his spear and threw it with great vigour.
It shot through the air like a bolt of lightning,
but it was not Psoas Mestor meant to hit,   180
but an Argive fighter standing next to him,
Ardántor, the one son of Macónius,
who came to Troy thinking it would be a jaunt,
a break from the drudgery of tanning skins,
who at that moment should have been looking
but was not, and it cost him a spear in the head,
in one side, out the other, helmet flying,
body jolting, leaving his dear father
inconsolable for the rest of his life.

Said Priam's royal son, "Nine Argives this morning.   190
Yet I am no more of a man than you are."

Neither Trojan nor Argive men laughed at Mestor's words,

that prince who could spin humour out of horror.
Around him arose a chorus of silence,
as weary nobles stared at the dead man.

Said the son of nobody to Prince Mestor,
"Speech is a powerful lord, my lord, but watch me."

Mestor deigned no reply to the goatherd's son
but turned and vanished among the Trojans.

Said Meriones, "He's got a sharp tongue, that one."   200

Added a deep voice behind them, "And a nice prick."

Much did Psoas dwell on the unpleasant words
Prince Mestor of Troy had uttered to him.

"*I am no less of a man than you are*" (10): I went over this sentence several times in the original before I could believe what it was saying. I still doubted it—surely some words were missing that would wholly change the meaning—until I found Prince Mestor's sardonic echo of it, "Yet I am no more of a man than you are," repeated four times (60, 78, 161, 191). At the time, and still for two millennia at least, such a claim by a commoner made to a royal would be so radical as to be ludicrous, nearly unintelligible. Despite Prince Mestor's mirthful response, the lèse-majesté would have been deeply shocking, hence the response, expressed with marvelous concision, just two key words:

> *War stopped*, as those who were fighting stopped their battling
> and those who were resting stopped their talking. (12–13)

"*Is this how the cheesemaker got the mettle to seek out a highest-born who knew metal? . . . The gods know, but they always keep their secrets*" (37–38, 42): Psoas seeks Mestor, indeed, he hunts him down. Such brazenness leaves Homer speechless, literally. There is no instance in *The Iliad*, not a single one, of a man of low rank deliberately choosing to fight a man of high rank. Even crusty Thersites limits himself to railing against a man of high rank, slinging only words at Agamemnon. So socially and personally unthinkable is the idea of a poorly trained commoner attacking a skilled prince that Thersites the bard craftily ascribes it to Hades. "Why would Hades do that?" (28), he asks. And indeed, why would Hades "infect Psoas with such rage" (32)? I assumed Thersites would leave the question unanswered, just another inexplicable whim of the gods. But Psoas has actual grounds for resenting Prince Mestor, as we will find out.

"Whose mother was a split-eyed chameleon" (51): How quirky that the reference should be not to the creature's colour variability, that for which  it is best known, but rather to its capacity to work its two eyes independently. This is the third reference to a chameleon (see *The Arrival: The Good Country, the Walls of Troy*, page 77, line 149, and *How Men Die*, page 140, line 35).

"quaking with fear, sprays of shit loudly blasting out of his arse" (57–58): The image is highly unusual, if not unique in Greek epic. You see such things in Greek comedy, in Aristophanes, for example, where characters fart in terror. In his *Frogs*, a god even, Dionysus, soils himself from fright. But in the epic tradition, there is no other reference of which I am aware of a fighting soldier so overcome by fear that his bowels loosen. That reaction rather feels ultra-modern, a hallmark of the wars of the twentieth century, which became not only monstrously lethal but extraordinarily noisy—a combination to make anyone lose control, as many modern grunts have attested. Mestor's scatological taunt echoes a point made earlier, about the Trojan War's appalling violence (see footnote *The ordinary man's fear*, pages 101–102). There is authenticity to the detail.

"Come, dark-haired purple man, hero at words, dandy on the dance floor" (83–84): The Trojans were dark-haired, the Greeks, fair-haired. We don't know whether this was a general truth or a stereotype. The purple refers to Mestor's clothing. Kings, princes, and members of the royal family distinguished themselves by wearing the colour. This custom was widespread. Homer attests to it, as does the archaeological record—from Ugarit, for example. As for the "dandy on the dance floor", that suggests class resentment on Psoas's part. The son of nobody must earn his daily bread and does not have the time to perfect

his dancing skills, while the man in purple, who lives off him, has plenty of leisure time.

"but stork? Who eats stork? And really, **tortoises?"** (99): As I can attest personally, the magnificent white stork, truly an avian airship, is still a sight to be seen in southern Europe and Turkey, a thrill to the North American eye.

As for tortoises, to this day, if a visitor strays onto the grassy fields around the ruins of Troy, trying to imagine a great fortified citadel, they may well be startled by motion underfoot and see a large tortoise, only slightly smaller than a bowler hat, dashing away. It dashes until it freezes and does its tortoise thing, at which point it can easily be picked up and examined. They're heavy, and they look impressively ancient. I wish the ones I encountered might have spoken and set the record straight, revealing what had actually happened at Hisarlik. But they only glared at me with their black eyes. And despite coming in a convenient shape, a sort of poke bowl with stumpy legs, they looked entirely unappetizing.

"cups of Pramnian wine spiced with onions, grated goat's cheese, and white barley" (107–108): Not your usual Cab Sav. It's interesting to note that for all of Homer's mentions of "wine-dark" seas, the Trojan War was a sober affair, with alcohol playing only a devotional or a nutritional role (as here—what a

concoction). There is no instance in *The Iliad* of men displaying drunkenness. Hence perhaps why the Greeks and the Trojans were so inexorably lucid about their predicament: because they had no escape, no relief.

"*Psnotnose . . . Psmallbrain . . . Pslowfat*" (44, 96, 110): I have tried to translate Mestor's mocking alterations of Psoas's name with equivalent silliness.

"***Do you think that just because it's on a spit we don't recognize the shape of a human arm, the fingers tightly curled***" (117–119): This allegation of cannibalism is unique in the Trojan War traditions. If true—and it is only an accusation on Mestor's part—it would speak to the calamitous conditions of the Greeks at Troy. And as with the bitter observation made earlier about the Greek fighters on the battlefield—"we were pigs" (see *The Wealth of Troy*, page 131, lines 7–8)—it makes me wonder about Thersites the bard's judgement. What Greek audience would want to hear such unsavoury truths about their own kind?

"***Come then, shrub-man, come strike at the sun above you***" (168): This is likely a belittling reference to Psoas's breastplate of wood stitched on linen. If Meriones, earlier, had stood in his military attire "as bright as gems" next to the dun-coloured son of nobody (see "*Well, there he is*", page 170, line 179), then a prince of Troy, the scion of a fabulously wealthy and sophisticated family and city, must indeed have shone like the sun.

"exposing his prick, which flopped down and dangled" (176): Explicitly sexual references, especially gay ones, are absent in the rest of the Trojan War tradition. That Achilles and Patroclus are lovers is an assumption that arises naturally from the story and helps explain Achilles' overwhelming grief and rage when Patroclus is killed by Hector. But Homer seeks to quash the notion when he awkwardly inserts unnecessary details about sleeping arrangements:

> And Achilles slept in the innermost part of the hut;
> by his side lay a woman whom he had taken from Lesbos,
> Phorbas's daughter, beautiful Diomédē.
> Patroclus lay near the opposite wall, and he too
> had a woman lying beside him, the lovely Iphis,
> a gift from Achilles after he captured Scyros. (9.663–668)

We get it, Homer. But why wouldn't the young men cavort with each other, if they were so inclined? You're young and tomorrow you may die, so why not savour it all, the beautiful male body, with its hardness, the beautiful female body, with its wetness? Love belongs to the mouth. And why are they sharing quarters otherwise?

Though alien to the Homeric tradition, Mestor's curious gesture is not alien to the later Greek tradition. As in all things Greek, so old, deep, and studied is the culture, there's a name for the deliberate exposing of one's genitals: *anasyrma*. Anasyrma was usually a gesture made by women. The best-known example concerns Demeter, the goddess of the harvest, after she has lost her daughter, Persephone, taken to the Underworld by Hades. Furious at Zeus for allowing such a thing to happen, Demeter leaves Olympus and wanders the earth disguised as an old woman, utterly bereft, a goddess in the throes of acute grief. She comes to Eleusis, where she is received by old Baubo and her husband Dysaulus, who try to comfort her. But Demeter, like Macónius above, is inconsolable. She sits on a stool, refusing food or drink, stock-still and stone-faced, overwhelmed by sorrow. According to the Orphic tradition, Baubo reacts by pulling up her skirt and showing her sex to the goddess. Demeter is astonished and bursts out laughing, a deep, regenerative belly laugh. It's important to note that the obscene gesture is not done for Baubo's gratification, but rather to have an effect on the goddess, to connect with her; it is a hallowed obscenity. And it works. Demeter's fecund laugh presages the fertility she will bring back to the scorched earth once she's agreed on a visitation schedule with Hades, of which the seasons of the earth are the manifest echoes, spring and summer when Persephone is with her above ground, fall and winter when she is away in the Underworld.

It is not clear what Thersites the bard has in mind with Mestor's anasyrma. A low reading would be that the prince is being disdainful. But his anasyrma could just as well be a sacred reminder of what the men are fighting for: that life-affirming fertility within us all, both physical and emotional, that the war is putting in such peril.

"Speech is a powerful lord" (197): "Daddy, tell me a story."

Yes, yes, my darling Helen. Let me sing Greek epic to you. I hope you like this next one, my little scholar.

Prince Mestor Tells Psoas How Helen Came to Troy

Said the prince to the son of nobody,
"Beware of news that comes from afar, Psoas.
Your poor senses are not equipped for it.
Your eyes, for example, what they take in.
You can see me in front of you, who shortly
will kill you, you can see the fierce men around us,
who are killing fierce men around us, you can see
the great, insurmountable walls of Troy
behind me, while I can make out the unkempt camp
you unwashed Argives have called home for ten years—   10
but how much more can you see beyond that?
You can see usefully only about
as far as an arrow can fly. After that,
the world becomes a blur, the details lost.

Your ears do worse than your eyes, as does your nose—
beyond a short distance they sense nothing at all.
Touch is for the blind—you must grope and fumble—
while taste is a useless sense, worse, a liar.
Any news that comes from beyond the horizon
can't be trusted because your senses cannot judge.   20
It might be true, but it could just as well be false.
Distance only distorts and confuses.
Distance will make you believe in lies, while the truth
right before your eyes is ignored. Best to trust
only what is within reach of your senses,
that which your brain can feed upon directly.
Then you live like you should, local and content.
Instead, if you feed upon the foreign,
you become a stressed fool, a sleepless dolt.

"For example, you were tricked by your kings,   30
not just the sons of Atreus, Menelaus,

and Agamemnon, but all of your kings.
They plotted and took you in right at the start,
and ten years on you're still dying for their lies.
Let me tell you the truth that distance has masked.
This is how the story goes, this is what happened.
Lord Tyndareus was king of Sparta,
and a mighty and magnificent man was he.
You only had to look at his four children
to see and know what their father was like.   40
By his queen, lovely Leda, he had two daughters,
you know their names, Helen and Clytemnestra,
and a pair of brawny twin sons, equally famed,
Castor and Pollux. The four so dazzled
mortal eyes that many suspected a god
had slipped in betwixt the king and his queen.
From an early age, word of Helen's beauty spread.
At the sight of her, eyes froze and tongues failed.
How could such fine features be, of face and figure,

of voice and movement? Upon meeting her, 50
a man was possessed by deep loneliness.
Then she spoke, and he came back to joyful life.
Such attention, such kindness, such humour.
Now the man not only stared, but smiled with thanks.
I know of what I speak, I see her every day.
She is my sister-in-law, my brother's wife.
Helen of Troy is the city's second sun.
Even as a girl she attracted suitors
and problems. Once, she was carried away
by Theseus, King of Athens. Well, right away, 60
without a moment's delay, her enraged brothers
marched out, sacked the city, and brought her back.
Tyndareus was a wise and careful man.
He wed Helen's sister, Clytemnestra,
to Agamemnon, King of Mycenae.
There, the Houses of Sparta and Mycenae
were united in an indefectible bond.

But what of ravishing Helen? Where might she go?
Eager suitors travelled from far and wide,
great and powerful kings all, wishing not only   70
her but the useful alliance with Sparta.
What's the version you were made to believe?
Ah yes: Menelaus got the Spartan king's nod.
To him would go the fair bride. Lucky man.
But think for a second, Psoas, you witless runt.
Why would Tyndareus give his last daughter
to the same family from the same city,
two brothers taking home his two daughters?
To marry off one seals an alliance,
to marry off two begs for a takeover.   80
But so the story goes. The sons of Atreus
got all the daughters of Tyndareus,
and they would have lived happily ever after,
if not for a dastardly Trojan prince.

"You were told that Paris took Helen away
against her will, because why, otherwise,
would an Argive queen flee with the umpteenth son
of a barbarian king, abandoning
husband, daughter, father, brothers, and country?
It's all the fault of that chance-met charmer and rake. 90
Nonsense! Do you hear me, Argive dumbhead? *Nonsense!*
Those two married in a good and proper wedding,
with her and her royal kinsfolk's full assent.
What a match! The Houses of Sparta and Troy
were united in an indefectible bond.
Whatever else you've heard is lies upon lies.
What, Paris arrives in a foreign city
with a small retinue and abducts a king's wife?
Not only that, he steals the treasury, too?
Not a single attendant raises the alarm? 100
Not a single guard cracks open an eyelid?
How quiet can an escaping treasury be?

How quiet can an unwilling, kidnapped wife be?
How quiet can stolen horses and carts be?
And this whole convoy stealthily gets to the coast,
a trip of some five leagues? No one catches them?
No one sets out after them on land or at sea?
The story goes that Menelaus was away.
How convenient. But what about Castor and Pollux?
Where were her combative, protective brothers?   110
Where *are* her combative, protective brothers?
Why are they not at Troy? Are we to believe
that for the exact same offence they would wage war
against the fellow king of Athens, but nothing
against the dandy prince of a lesser race?
If Helen's brothers were that weak and fickle,
they would not be as widely famed as they are.

"Then, to complete this ludicrous fable,
Paris returns home and to his righteous father

cheerfully announces, 'My trip went very well. 120
I was received by King Menelaus
most graciously, and so, when he departed,
in return, I absconded with his treasury—
see the heavy chests there—and, while at it,
I also stole his hot wife. There she stands,
just a little battered and bruised. In a moment,
I will remove her chains and hood, if not her gag,
and you will see what a great catch she is.'
And in this fantastical version of events,
King Priam, Queen Hecuba, thoughtful Hector, 130
every brother and sister, the whole family,
we all slapped Paris on the back, gleeful, and said,
'Well done! Good fun! Now let us prepare for a war
that will likely wipe us off the face of the earth.'

"Let me tell you what really happened, Psoas,
so that you might know the truth before you die.

Yes, suitors from all over came to Sparta,
one valorous king after another.
Menelaus, Diomédes, Ajax,
Idómeneus, Odysseus, besides   140
many kings and princes from further shores.
Much they feasted at Tyndareus's court,
but the king was game because the cause was good.
Beautiful Helen was courted by every man,
each trying to win her heart and her father's nod.
Then arrived Paris, with a great show of wealth,
because ambassadors, as you wouldn't know,
don't travel like beggars in rags, at least
not prince ambassadors from sacred Troy.
Right away Paris made an impression.   150
He showered Tyndareus, Leda, Castor,
Pollux, and Helen with sumptuous gifts
that the other suitors together could not match.
And Paris is strikingly handsome, too,

graceful and unnervous, with a charming smile
(I know that smile, it runs in the family),
a match to Helen's incomparable beauty.
That is how we like it here, to be surrounded
by beauty, hence why Helen fits so well with us.
While the Argive kings were like so many   160
grunting boars lifting their snouts from the mud,
Paris was a proper prince, paying every heed
yet standing his ground, fully and naturally
himself while in a foreign land. It was with ease
that he slipped into the daughter's glad heart
and won the king's and two brothers' high esteem.
Tyndareus sought counsel and consulted seers.
All—the words of men, the entrails of animals,
the flight paths of birds, the dreams of those who see—
spoke with one voice: Helen should be with Paris.   170
The union is blessed by the gods, who love
peace and beauty, who love Sparta and Troy.

The king himself could only see advantages.
Here he was, respected and well allied,
with Castor and Pollux to succeed him
as mighty co-kings of Sparta, and here now
was the prospect of an alliance with Priam.
His power and wealth were not just fabled:
every season, ships from Laconia
traded with Troy, to mutual benefit.   180
And if he rejected Paris and instead
gave Helen to, say, Diomédes, then what?
He would have two neighbouring sons-in-law with eyes
on his throne, Agamemnon and Diomédes,
with daughter pitted against daughter, because that
is the scorpion way of your countrymen.
Better to give no Argive suitor cause for war
and at the same time secure a powerful friend.
Troy would no doubt come to Sparta's help, if need be.
Priam's word could be trusted, that was well known.   190

And his daughter seemed so happy, there was that, too.
What a nice pair they were, the two of them,
like two birds in a nest. And so the old king
came to his decision, the smiles of his daughter
blinding him to the scowls of her other suitors.

"The wedding of Paris and Helen went forth,
and a truly splendid affair it was,
with rejoicing on the part of mortals and gods,
or so Tyndareus the mortal thought,
but he and his sons did not catch the bitter   200
words exchanged between stuffed mouthfuls of sweet
food by the spurned suitors, or the ironic
smiles of the gods, who all knew how the sad
tale would spin out, nor did they hear of the evil
plot hatched as the suitors danced to the lively
music, or up on Olympus the knowing
nods of the gods, who all knew how the sad

tale would spin out. Of all the hopeful kings,
Menelaus was the suitor who brooded
the most over the failure of his suit. 210
Was it his heart, loin, or purse that was most aching?
His older brother Agamemnon did not care.
He was more concerned about the danger
of Priam interfering in Argive affairs.
If something happened to Castor and Pollux,
would the Trojan brother-in-law sue for the crown,
his beautiful Spartan queen at his side?
What a disaster that would be. And so,
the two brothers began to incite and goad.
Was it not an outrage that the most prized woman 220
among them had been dangled before their eyes,
only to be given to a foreign fop?
Was there an Argive man who did not hate Paris?
The spurned suitors agreed that, one and all,
they had been treated with contempt by Sparta's king.

What an old fool, he! The outrage could not go
unanswered, not if they valued their honour.
Some of the suitors perhaps nursed a broken
heart over the loss of Helen, while others
might truly have seen a collective insult, 230
while still others guessed that they might profit
from the outrage, and then there were those, as always
in the affairs of men, who just followed along.
Whatever the reason—ache or greed or
native stupidity—as the newlyweds
sailed away, bedecked in garlands of flowers,
happy as could be, their royal kinsfolk
waving from the pier as their subjects cheered
from the shore and the immortals watched keenly
from Olympus, already the short wick 240
of their happiness was nearly burned out,
already the schemers were hatching their plot
to steal and make their own the throne of Sparta.

"They would spare the old king—even better,
he would be brought around. The main obstacle
was not the memory of people who had seen
with their eyes, heard with their ears, and celebrated
with their throats. No, that's never a problem.
Nothing corrects an error of memory
like the blade of a sword. It was not Paris   250
who married Helen—what a foolish notion.
Who paid you to spread that lie? Or did the wine
go to your weak brain and mist your feeble eyes?
It was the second son of Atreus,
Menelaus of Mycenae, who wed her. Got it?
Stick to the truth, or your head will roll to the ground.
That's how you take care of the hoi polloi.
The main obstacle to their heinous scheme
was Helen's fearsome brothers, Castor and Pollux,
two foes that no sane man would dare take on   260
face to face. Look how Theseus had paid

for his abduction of their sister, his life
barely spared, his city left in ruins.
The twins would have to be taken by stealth.
Why, look at this gift from gracious Paris
to Menelaus, a most powerful bow,
with its quiver of fine, iron-tipped arrows.
Look at their feather fletching, so distinctive.
No one in these lands has arrows like these.

"So it came to pass one night: Tyndareus   270
spent time with his Achaean son-in-law,
Agamemnon. A most pleasant conversation
they had until the King of Mycenae
took his leave when his brother came in turn
to speak nicely with the King of Sparta.
Suddenly, the two men heard a hue and a cry,
shrieks to chill the soul. 'What is it?' cried the old king.

"Agamemnon came in, ashen-faced. 'Lord,'
said he, 'I never thought such treachery
was possible. Their ships have only just left!' 280

" 'Of what do you speak? Make your meaning plain.
Has something happened to dear Helen and Paris?'

" 'Worse, and closer to home. Your brave sons are dead,
both of them felled by the arrows of a traitor!'

"And so king and king and king's brother hurried
to see the work of one king and his brother
against another king whose heart would never mend.
One arrow had struck Castor in the back,
so he never saw the coward who felled him,
Menelaus it was, while another arrow 290
struck Pollux in the throat, so that he could not
speak the name of the coward who felled him,

Agamemnon it was. The sons of Atreus
led old Tyndareus to see their work,
the bodies of his beloved twin sons.

" 'Look, look!' they said. 'The arrows—they are Trojan!
He has left but two days and already
he has set his treacherous plan into action.
But Paris is only a pretty puppet.
The hand of his ignoble father guides him.   300
Priam wants to rule these lands and has chosen
to start with Sparta. We can't let this happen!'

"Agamemnon fell on one knee and clasped
old Tyndareus's hand. Said he to him,
'Lord king of Sparta, I am your son-in-law.
I love you and your daughter Clytemnestra
as I loved your sons, more than I love myself.
I beseech you, let me avenge this evil deed.

I will make the Trojans pay with their blood,
every drop, for what they have done to us.'   310

"Next, Menelaus fell on one knee and clasped
old Tyndareus's other hand. Said he to him,
'Lord king of Sparta, I am not your son-in-law,
though I ardently wished to be. I love you
and your daughter Helen as I loved your sons,
more than I love myself. I beseech you,
let me avenge this evil deed with my brother.
We will make the Trojans pay with their blood,
every drop, for what they have done to us.'

"Never has love turned so quickly to hate   320
as Tyndareus's love for Paris did.
Through his tears, before his sons' bloodied bodies,
said he to Menelaus, 'She is yours!
What a fool I was not to see through his deceit.

Paris is my daughter's husband no more,
and she never was. By royal decree,
I make her yours. You are Helen's husband,
Menelaus. You are my son-in-law.
The Houses of Sparta and Mycenae
are united in an indefectible bond. 330
And now go—*go!* You have my blessing, my dear sons.
Sail to Troy and free my Helen. Kill Priam,
kill Paris, make the Trojans pay with their blood,
every drop, for what they have done to us.
Now I must grieve my lost sons, my dear sons.'

" 'You have spoken wisely, Tyndareus,'
said Agamemnon. 'My brother and I,
with all the other leaders of our land,
who all love you dearly, will set sail for Troy.
We will punish the city like your sons 340
punished Theseus when he stole Helen,

only worse. I assure you, we will do far worse.
Not a man, woman, or child will we spare,
not a house or wall will we leave standing.
Troy will be wiped off the face of the earth,
and we will bring back your precious daughter,
my brother's rightful wife, and all the treasures
that Paris stooped to steal when he stole her
(for that, too, the fiendish brothers had done,
murdered with one hand while with the other,   350
on the same night, they stole from the treasury).
Before the year is over, she will be back,
I assure you, and next to a proud Spartan king
will sit a proud Spartan queen, as should be.'

"And so Agamemnon rose to his feet,
now the commander-in-chief of an armada,
and so Menelaus rose to his feet,
now the rightfully married husband of Helen,

dastardly liars who were happy to drag
a good man and his city to war for their gain. 360
The old king nodded and went off to grieve his sons.
Note how he did not catch Agamemnon's
blunder. Of what proud Spartan king was he speaking?
Sparta still had a king. But grief and old age
had quite broken Tyndareus's spirit,
and soon enough, following the advice
of his trusted sons-in-law, he gave way
to his only heir, the crownless Menelaus.

"Our ears and eyes on the ground—for that is how
we Trojans learn the truth, through real observation— 370
have told us of yet another preposterous
twist to this baldly fake tale: there's a daughter
to the fake royal pair. A touchless conception—
how delicate of Menelaus to spare
his new consort his laughable ugliness.

Who is this Hermione? Where did she come from?
We hear that she was plucked from a family
slaughtered during a raiding expedition,
destined to be a slave, only to see herself
suddenly elevated to king's daughter. 380
Lucky her! She won't disprove the story,
will she? No, no. Menelaus is her daddy,
and she wants to see her mummy Helen again,
whom she misses terribly. In the meantime,
her adoring doddering grandpa dotes on her.

"Argive kings tumbled over each other
to join the scheme, a noble few moved, perhaps,
by Argive pride, but most moved by Argive greed.
Every king who was there swore that it was so,
that Menelaus had married Helen 390
only to have her stolen by Paris,
while those who weren't there believed the whole tale.

They trusted and they hungered. What king could resist
the lure of glory and the spoils of war?

"That is what happened, but how would you know?
All you heard were the words of your leaders
telling of events you had never witnessed.
Words born beyond the border of the senses
all have the same good taste to the gullible mind.
But now they taste bitter, don't they, Psoas? 400
What of that quick, gainful war promised by your kings?

"Are you surprised, then, that we were so indignant
when Argive emissaries came to us
with their outrageous request that we return
lawfully wedded Helen, joy and pride
not only of Paris but of our whole city?
Even more scandalous: we were ordered
to pay compensation far in excess

of the paltry dowry Helen had brought.
To lie is one thing, but then to ask the lied-to　　　410
to believe the lies shows despicable gall.

"Are you surprised, then, that every Trojan,
every man, woman, and child, cried the same reply:
'No! We will not return our darling Helen!'
And we have held steadfast these ten long years
because we know Paris did nothing wrong.
If he had, do you think we would have put up
with all this suffering, with all this loss?
A thief does not die for the sake of his theft.
Enough! There is not a shred of truth to the tale　　　420
of the abduction of Helen by Paris.
You trusted more than what your eyes could see
and believed more than what your ears could hear.
Now you will die. That is the price you will pay
for feeding on lies, son of nobody."

Mestor turned his eyes to the gentle, cloudless sky,
and the war spirit seemed to leave the prince.
Said he to the son of nobody, "This morning
I spent some time with my youngest, a boy.
He is the sweetest of all my children, 430
a joyful creature of song and sunlight,
bright of eyes and bright of smile. He is five
and he is a child of this war, damn you,
like all his siblings. He has never set foot
outside the city walls. I hope one day
to walk out with him and bring him to the sea,
so that he might run and play in its waves.
I'd like to do that, the gods be willing."

The prince raised his sword and moved forward two steps.
The son of nobody retreated a pace. 440
Would Psoas be true to his fighting words,
and would he now attack the Trojan prince?

Men watched, as the two stared at each other fiercely.

Mestor turned and vanished among the Trojans.

"*Distance will make you believe in lies, while the truth right before your eyes is ignored*" (23–24): "Mr. Harlow, what are you doing?"

"My work."

"What's this? How do these fragments go together? This is an offence not only against fibre but against grammar! What on earth are you thinking?"

"Well, indeed, the writer makes mistakes. But look, from this angle, the fragments arranged like so, one can make out the—"

"No, no, no!"

"Yes, yes, yes!"

"Nonsense!"

"I disagree."

"There's nothing there."

"It's right here."

"No it's not."

"Let me show you."

"DON'T PRESUME TO TEACH ME MY JOB, YOU PUPPY!"

"Sir, I can't take this anymore! The work you've given me is so mind-numbingly boring. It's like fishing in the Pacific with a single hook. For every one little sardine we catch, there's a hundred million tons of empty salt water. Who really cares about Oxyrhynchus? There's a good reason why ordinary people are forgotten by history: it's because they're mostly forgettable. You want a citizen of Oxyrhynchus? Look out the window. You see that man in the blue anorak? Or that woman about to enter the coffee shop? They too pay bills and go grocery shopping, and I wish them well—but do I care to see his tax return or her grade three report card? We're all citizens of Oxyrhynchus, hopeful and humdrum. This godforsaken pile of papyrus is mostly a Mount Everest of banality. Whereas with Homer, you get the essential, you get a big fat whale, all the red blood and rich blubber of lived life—and he's beached right there, at hand, complete in twenty-four books, not obliterated by the shredder of Father Time. What I've done is search for the dreams of the Oxyrhynchites, that which made them bigger than themselves, their secret immortalities. And if one looks carefully, one can find them. So these fragments here, if you—"

"What—what—*WHAT ARE YOU SAYING?!* I cannot believe my ears. I—I—"

"Professor Cubitt, please put your cane down!"

It all came crashing down.

"a trip of some five leagues" (106): A league is approximately five kilometres or three miles, so Paris and his booty would have had to travel about twenty-five kilometres or fifteen miles.

"**Where** *are her combative, protective brothers? Why are they not at Troy?*" (111–112): Good questions. Homer, through Helen, notes the absence of Castor and Pollux, then directly explains it:

> "But two commanders I look for and I don't see:
> Castor and Pollux, my mother's sons, my dear brothers.
> Either they didn't come here from Lacedæmon,
> or else, though they came, they haven't entered the fighting
> because of the insults and shame I have brought upon them."
> So she thought. But already the life-giving earth
> lay piled up over them in their beloved country. (3.236–244)

But why are they dead? Who killed them? Where Homer is silent, Thersites accuses: Helen's dear brothers are not at Troy because they were murdered by the two royal brothers from Mycenae, who then made the most outrageous claims, Menelaus that he was Helen's wronged husband, and Agamemnon, her righteously indignant brother-in-law.

"*He showered Tyndareus, Leda, Castor, Pollux, and Helen with sumptuous gifts*" (151–152): As I believe many writers do with their words, I took to reading *The Psoad* aloud as I worked on it. At first it felt awkward. My accent, my diction. How did bards do it? But I slowed my delivery, inhabited each word, took on the role. The mirror of my wardrobe proved useful. I began to sing. I might have been in an open-air theatre in Ancient Greece, not a shabby room at Magdalen. Then, after hearing myself recite, I sat down and determined where the English-language sun failed to shine as brightly as it might on the Trojan landscape. To edit Ancient Greek song—I've never done anything that so twined together every aspect of my being and brought me such joy.

"*He showered Tyndareus, Leda, Castor, Pollux, and Helen with sumptuous gifts*" (151–152): What do you think, Helen? Did you like this fragment? Oh, what evil liars, Agamemnon and Menelaus, according to Thersites the bard. But don't worry: their wickedness will not go unpunished.

"*nor did they hear of the evil plot hatched as the suitors danced to the lively music*" (204–206): [*ring*]
[*ring*]
"Hello?"
I had just left the Papyrology Work Room, was crossing the marbled lobby of the Ancient World Library, had turned on my phone.
"Harlow! Why haven't you been answering my calls or my texts?!"
It was Gail, on a voice call.

"*That is what happened, but how would you know?*" (395): It is stating the obvious to say that this telling of how Helen got to Troy is at variance with the prevailing Trojan War tradition, which has it that whether she came willingly as a lover or unwillingly as a resigned captive, she nevertheless came in a manner that was illicit and unsanctioned, that Paris was wined and dined in Sparta, then stole the Spartan king's wife and money. This is how Homer has it, and also the author of the now-vanished *Cypria,* one of the other books in the Epic Cycle. Such behaviour would be an outrage at any time to any people, but would have been an especially egregious abuse to the Ancient Greeks, who took the rules of hospitality very seriously, and would explain their unbounded fury and the tremendous efforts they made to reclaim Helen and exact revenge on the Trojans.

What has been less clear to listeners and readers throughout the ages is why the Trojans tolerated Paris's disgraceful behaviour. Why value a stolen wife and a bit of treasure over an entire city and the life of its inhabitants? One could postulate that the Trojans, imbued with their own wealth and power, thought at first that they could get away with it, that the Greeks would complain but ultimately do nothing. But once they heard that the Greeks were mustering the largest armada ever assembled in the history of the world, that a war was well and truly on, why didn't they promptly send Helen packing? Why did they hold on to her for ten years of ruinous war leading to the destruction of their city and their own mass murder? The insanity of it, like all insanities, is baffling.

Our modern tendency is to rationalize myth away and inject realism. It's a phenomenon we also see with the story of Jesus, whose miracle-laden narrative jars with our scientific way of thinking. To give only three examples concerning the Trojan War, we have Dares the Phrygian's *History of the Fall of Troy*, Dictys the Cretan's *Journal of the Trojan War*, and Quintus of Smyrna's *The Fall of Troy*. All three are much later works, have a gritty I-was-there feel, and are markedly less magical. In each, the incredible is replaced by the sensible. In the duel between Menelaus and Paris, for example, where Homer has the goddess Aphrodite save Paris in a swirl of heavy mist, magically transporting him back to Troy, in both Dares and Dictys, it is Hector, using his brawn and his bronze, who saves Paris.

The temptation is to see truth in the rational and mere embellishment in the myth. But every belief system tends to be self-reinforcing. Ask a silly/Marxist/religious/reasonable/deluded person a question, and you'll likely get a silly/Marxist/religious/reasonable/deluded answer. Myth requires open systems of understanding, and inquiry into it must take into account its nature, and the nature of myth has both reasonable and unreasonable elements. It is a limited venture to examine the unreasonable with a reasonable eye. To do so is potentially to miss the essential.

Mestor's version of how Helen came to Troy feels like a rationalization. It is certainly more credible from the Trojan perspective—it explains why they resisted the Greeks to their collective dying breath. But his story actually only shifts the burden of insanity onto the Greek side. Why fight for so many years for the sake of a lie that finally wins them only one woman and no treasure? Why didn't the Greek kings, after a while, just give up and cut their losses?

Either way, the stubbornness of the Greeks and Trojans is hubris on a cataclysmic scale, insanity breeding insanity, until everything is lost, a joint civilizational suicide that led to the wiping out of Troy and, soon after, to the collapse of Mycenaean Greece. But this is how ancient stories go: they're stark, violent, crazy, deeply disturbing. It's not just the Trojan War. Think of Oedipus, Antigone, the Orestes. Think of Gilgamesh. Think of the Bible.

It's hard to imagine that a Greek audience would like to hear such a poor character reference for Agamemnon and Menelaus. Even Greek authors of the Classical period who agreed that the desire for profit was a major motivator of the war also argued that the Greeks were nonetheless defending their honour.

As for how Helen got to Troy, as mentioned earlier, there is no historical proof of the existence of any of the characters of the Trojan War and only slight evidence of friction between the Greeks and the Trojans. In a word, it's all fiction. Does it make sense, then, to quibble about which fiction is truer? Was Little Red Riding Hood's garment actually red—or was it possibly green? If we want only on-the-ground, actual factual, historical facts, we should find a big window high up and throw all the Trojan War out, besides many other stories from yesteryear, including the Gospels. We have no idea how Helen got to Troy. The determinant must finally be the reader's desire, how the reader wants to interpret the story. How do you want Helen to get to Troy?

Once more, the story of the Trojan War and the story of Jesus are very similar: distant, immediate, unverifiable, compelling, subjective.

"I spent some time with my youngest" (429): "Daddy, when are you coming home? I miss you."

You said that a few times, Helen. What had Professor Cubitt said to me? *Go home, man, go home.*

"a joyful creature of song and sunlight" (431): "I'm at the hospital! Something's wrong with Helen," Gail said.

"What?"

"I said, I'm at the hospital, in the emergency."

"I heard you. What's wrong with her? I thought you said it was just a fever and a cough."

"It got worse really quickly. She couldn't breathe, she was going purple. She's right in front of me. There are doctors all over her. I'm so fucking scared, Harlow."

"Mestor turned and vanished among the Trojans" (444): The repetition of this line (see *Psoas Threatens Prince Mestor*, page 190, line 199) leads me to think that Psoas and Mestor met up on the battlefield over the course of many weeks, perhaps months, each time getting closer and closer to actual combat. The fragment that follows, Oxyrhynchus-stitched, must come after one such bristling encounter, Mestor's words being the cause of Psoas's extraordinary reaction.

"Mestor turned and vanished among the Trojans" (444): I could feel myself fade, the life in me bleaching in the springtime English sun.

Thersites Speaks to Psoas

Thersites came up to the son of nobody,
there, not far from the banks of the Scamander,
and said he to him, "Psoas, hello? *Hello?*
I am speaking to you. You went dog-mad
with Prince Mestor of Troy just now. I never saw
any warrior do what you just did,
even heroes like god-blooded Achilles
or storming Ajax or fearless Diomédes.
What did he say that made you go crazy?
Are you listening, Psoas? I watched it all   10
and this is what I saw. You were standing there
behind your shield, in a stupor it seemed.
It's as if you were waiting to be slain.
I don't know what revived you, certainly not

our shouting, but suddenly you did revive—
and you went mad! You looked around, ignoring us,
gazing thither and yon, and then you bolted
for the enemy line. A foe barred your way,
ready for the fight, no less than mighty
Sandros of Lydia, son of Xanthelus, 20
a killer of many brave Argive men.
Did you hurl your spear at him? No, you had none.
Did you attack him with your sword? No, you did not.
Did you at least shout at him? No, none of that.
You simply marched up to him, ignoring
his brandished spear and his menacing scowl,
and you shoved him aside with your poxy shield,
knocking him off his feet. It was not brave,
cunning, or hot-blooded—it was just *rude*.
We're here to fight and kill like warriors, 30
not push and shove like schoolboys. Then you turned left—
and ran behind the enemy line in plain view.

By the way, I seized that moment when Sandros
lay sprawled on the ground, astounded at what you'd done—
the outrage!—to pick him off with my spear,
a quick, easy jab through the face. I do believe
his noisy death distracted the Trojans
around him, who might otherwise have turned
to warn their comrades about your intrusion.
So don't forget, Psoas: I, Thersites,   40
helped you in your idiotic enterprise.

"But I don't mean to intrude my humble self,
fighter of great repute though Sandros was.
Now, Psoas, think about this for a moment,
ponder this question: in battle, who is my foe?
In some cases, I hear my foe's enmity,
a strange tongue that goes with a certain tint of skin
or a peculiar type of helmet or weapon.
Troy is an impressive spice rack of speeches.

They say there is not a language on earth 50
that the Trojans do not speak. Every child of theirs
acquires a new language by each birthday,
Luvian by year one, their native tongue.
By year two, their children speak Nesite, of course,
and so it goes, years three, four, five, six, onwards,
Palaic, Lycian, Milyan, Carian,
Phrygian, Mysian, Pisidian,
Lydian, Akkadian, Aethiopian,
Hurrian, Aegyptian, until they run out.
And alas for us, the Trojans are much loved 60
in this world, and each tongue comes attached to a man
with a sword. So, much gibberish in the fight.
But the Trojans, my enemies in the main?
Any man who can speak good Luvian,
without mistakes, is not likely my ally.
But some of us Argives speak Luvian, too,
since, after all, before we fought with the Trojans,

we traded with them. We exchanged not only goods
but words. And Troy, being a city of the world,
has many citizens who speak excellent Greek, 70
often better than some native Argives.
We would do well if some of our comrades switched sides
so that we might kill them. Sever the head,
save the tongue, I say. Takes those Arcadians—
my grandfather used to speak something like that,
but he was a lonely, half-crazed shepherd who
never left his meadow. It's goats who taught him Greek.
Language is no help in distinguishing
who my enemy is. Left to themselves,
languages never go to war. All they do is 80
breed like rabbits, producing strange new children.

"If not by his speech, perhaps I can recognize
my Trojan foe by his dress? Seems reasonable,
that two armies should be distinctly attired.

I would say that was the case some years ago,
when we first arrived to wage war on this cursed plain.
These Trojans are fancy dressers by nature.
But after ten long years, it's all mixed up.
Take this helmet I'm wearing—it's Trojan.
I cleaned out the spilled brains and made it my own.   90
Why not? It's better than my old helmet,
which was also Trojan, as it happens,
but my helmet before that, it was Argive,
and it was torture, used to cut into me
here and here. We've all been through this routine,
every one of us. I kill one of theirs,
then go shopping. It's the commerce of war:
blood the coin, bronze the ware, bargains everywhere.
A man who stood in full battle gear, proud and fierce,
eyes flashing, becomes goods at the agora.   100
His armour, weapons, helmet, taslet, sandals,
even his soiled tunic, if it's quality—

it's all on sale, one day only. What fits well
and is better made, I quickly put on,
then trade the rest at the nightly market,
where every man is keen to resupply himself.
And the Trojans do exactly the same:
they kill and then rush to dress like the killed.
No surprise, then, that after ten years of war
we should fight in a ragbag mishmash of gear   110
earned, found, traded, or stolen, fighting a foe
who looks like us, wielding weapons that look like ours.
Only heroes are still distinctly tailored.
No hand-me-down chameleons are they.

"So I ask again, Psoas, who is my foe?
I'll tell you: my foe is the man in front of me.
That's it! The men beside me and behind me
must be my comrades-in-arms because I can't
fight from the side or the back. I can only fight

forward, so there is where I find my foe— 120
where my eyes can see and my arms can harm.

"In this scheme, my hated enemy is not—
I repeat to be clear, you clod, is *not*—
a single man running behind enemy lines
amidst thousands of men who hate his guts
and would happily kill him. We watched you run.
How will you survive? You won't, you can't, you'll die.

"Sandros knew you were behind enemy lines,
but I killed him before he could say a word.
Others saw you, too, Argive and Trojan, 130
but we all knew *here*, while you were over *there*,
moving fast, running like a zigzagging hare.
To the harried eye, you were just a man running,
and in a war there's a lot of running.
A foot soldier's main arms are his feet, hence the name.

Only you were Argive—but how could they know?
You were running faster than news could be shouted
and understood. 'There, that man there! Stop him!'
By the time a Trojan understood—'What? Who? Where?'—
you had moved on, you were too far, you were lost   140
in the warring crowd. Sharp-eyed Glaucus saw you.
He took aim and threw his spear. But hero
though he is, he missed. Dodging left and right
as you were—did fleet-footed Hermes lend you
his sandals?—he missed and killed one of his own,
Drakos, son of Haitol, a Carian potter
whose hands would never work soft clay again.
The spear hit him hard in the back and threw him
to the ground, where he ate a last meal of earth
as his blood poured out. Your next sorry man,   150
Arthanos of Zelea, an orphan,
didn't travel very far to come to war,
only the lush foothills of Mount Ida,

where he tended goats and made good cheese, like you.
Did he think you carried hot news, hence your speed?
You sliced his head off in one mighty stroke.
That trusting soul was so surprised that his body
continued to stand as his helmeted head
hit the ground with a clang. Onwards you ran.
Eumodrax the Paphlagonian you brought down   160
by stabbing him in his generous stomach.
Never again would his many children
bounce on it as his loving wife looked on.
But—lo, what ho—you couldn't pull your sword out!
Quick in, clean out, I say. But not this one.
Big Eumodrax died hugging what killed him,
while you sprinted on, barehanded. What, fool,
is a sailor so pressed for time that he rushes
out to sea but forgets to board his ship?
This is a war! A war is fought with weapons.   170
You had none left. Was your plan to take on

the whole Trojan army in a boxing match?
You ran and ran and ran. There, below that small hill,
you ran deeper into Trojan territory.
Over there, you returned closer to the front line.
What directed your madness? You seemed to be blind
yet furiously looking. But at times you stopped.
We saw it. You stopped to talk to some Trojans.
Were you asking them questions? From our distant spot,
that seemed to be the nature of your meetings. 180
Were you a sightseer now, tootling about
the world, pausing to chat with the locals,
asking about the nearby sights? They seemed helpful,
as they pointed toward Troy. You raced off again.
Did they comment on how well you spoke Luvian,
with such a charming heavy Greek accent?

"You ran and ran and ran. If it was tiring
for your legs, imagine how tiring it was

---

for our eyes, following your mad frolic
across the Trojan plain. We lost you at times.   190
War is a crowd. We lost you behind people,
we lost you behind tents, and finally
we nearly lost you to distance. Were you
that speck running up to the Ilian Gate?
A man was ahead of you, sauntering home.
The light glinted off him. It was Prince Mestor.
You just missed him. The small door in the great gate
opened, and the royal stepped through. The door
closed just in time for you to kick it. What, Psoas,
were you trying to storm Troy all by yourself?   200

"You ran and ran and ran. Where now? Back to us,
picking up swords and spears along the way
and killing men as you ran, men whose names
I don't know because their faces I didn't see.
I only saw their stricken bodies falling.

You ran so fast you attacked like a hawk
striking from above, unseen by its victim,
breaking wings, scattering feathers, wrenching its prey
from the air before flying on. The last man
you killed, though, I do know his name. It was   210
Menacheon the Scythian, the second son
of Latos, a young man who will have no children
because he met you, a broad-shouldered fighter,
new to war but eager and good at it,
only unlucky. He'd hoped to prove his worth
and gain fame and glory. His body is right there.
He didn't see you coming from behind,
nor did he see you stab him through the head.
His left eye sailed out into the world like
a lonely little boat onto the ocean.   220
When you struck him, your spear was parallel
to the ground, then, as he shuddered and fell forward,
it turned perpendicular, like a staff,

and like a staff you used it as you walked
over him, as if he were a bridge, slipping in
between two surprised Trojans back into our midst.
As you angled the spear forward, his helmet
came off and the top of his head cracked open.
Lo! His brain fell out, looking as startled
as a poor tortoise wrenched out of its shell. 230
Menacheon lifted himself onto all fours,
then heaved himself back so that he was sitting,
holding his brain in his helmet, staring at it
with his one good eye, then gazing up at his friends.
When he realized that he was dead, sorry
Menacheon, the second son of Latos,
wept one cycle loudly, then fell forward.
It was madness. And, great Zeus, the look on your face!
Medusa's would be a softer sight. I'm glad
we're on the same side, because otherwise 240
I'd die of fright just looking at you. In fact,

didn't I just see—no, I shall not name him,
it was only a momentary weakness—
didn't I just see one of our brave men turn
and run at the sight of you? Psoas, *please blink!*"

"*You were standing there behind your shield, in a stupor it seemed*" (11–12): A citadel of bliss, bathed in the light of the Aegean Sea, collapsed. How poor words are at capturing the bottomless unhappiness of a life that has been blighted.

"*speak Nesite, of course*" (54): Nesite, now commonly called Hittite, was the language of the neighbouring empire, with which the Trojans had close commercial and political relations, sometimes tense.

"*No hand-me-down chameleons are they*" (114): What's with all the chameleons? I can see one in a storm, clinging to a branch, trying to survive, its soft skin blinking a kaleidoscope of colours, its eyes gyrating wildly.

"*War is a crowd*" (191): "I'll put you on video. I'll call you right back!" Gail said.
She hung up, I waited, she called back. She spoke in a rapid hush. "She wasn't feeling well. But it was just regular stuff. Then her breathing turned harsh and gurgly. So I called an ambulance. They raced us over here."
"Let me see, let me see!"
Gail switched the viewpoint on her phone and held it up. Life reduced to a screen two and a half inches by six. A cell phone as epicentre. She kept moving

it as events unfolded. Sometimes it was a wall I was staring at, sometimes people's legs.

What I saw, intermittently, was four or five men and women in scrubs working over you. You were lying on a metal table, medical machines beeping and blinking around you. I recognized the pyjamas you were wearing and your shoes. But I never got to see your face, not properly; it was obstructed by a big tube coming out of your mouth, taped to your cheek, and a doctor or a nurse—I couldn't tell who was what—was nearly always in the way. Curt instructions were followed by quick actions. A syringe flashed in the light. The tube in your mouth was replaced with another that seemed narrower. Sometimes your body jerked. I watched, trying to understand what was going on.

Then your mother dropped her phone. I was left staring at the ceiling of the emergency room, at squares of foam tile and neon lights.

"*Back to us . . . killing men as you ran*" (201, 203): Psoas openly crosses into enemy territory, wreaks havoc, then crosses back over to his side. Every hero in Homer has his *aristeia* ("outstanding performance"), in which he justifies his status as a hero, at the cost of many enemy lives. This is clearly Psoas's *aristeia*, the moment when the son of nobody shows his worth and becomes a hero. But the details aren't quite right. Despite mentions in *The Iliad* of Hector "foaming at the mouth" or Achilles being taken over by *lyssa* ("rabid rage"), the Homeric hero during his *aristeia* acts with strategic calculation, which shows itself in two ways. First, the hero does not act alone. He is with his comrades and his exploits come as the result of an opportunity created by them collectively on the battlefield, a favourable turn of events. The moment arises, as with the lifting of a curtain, and the hero, now centre stage, performs in words and in deeds. He earns glory and honour because of the compact between him and his comrades: he will *do* so long as they *witness* and *remember*. Second, the Homeric hero, when his time comes to shine, hedges his bets by taking on soft military targets. How do Diomédes, Agamemnon, Patroclus, and Achilles earn their military honours? By chasing after Trojan soldiers as they flee the battlefield in the grip of panic. It's hard to see real courage in that.

Compare the battle exploits of a Homeric hero with the actions, say, of a U.S. soldier in the Vietnam War who has thrown off his cumbersome helmet and flak jacket and raced on his own into the jungle, oblivious of the flying bullets. He accomplishes extraordinary deeds, killing any number of Vietcong. His comrades, lying flat in the grass, stare at him in amazement. His daring is astounding, his energy stunning. But he is not showing valour, he's actually lost his mind. The stress of battle has undone him, and he acts in psychological isolation and with disconnected impulsiveness. His outburst is suicidal. If he attacks the enemy, perhaps his sortie may prove militarily useful, but if he attacks civilians, it will not. And the insanity of his action will be obvious if he throws himself upon the corpse of an already dead enemy to mutilate it, or, in the worst case, if he attacks his own side.

Whom does Psoas more closely resemble, the Homeric hero or the Vietnam War soldier gone berserk?

"Psoas, **please blink!"** (245): I could hear tense voices but couldn't make out what the doctors were saying.

At one point, Gail quavered, "Will she be all right?"

"Gail! Gail! Pick your phone up off the floor, please! *GAIL!*"

Achilles Speaks to Psoas

"Men, the son of Peleus is approaching!"

Indeed, god-blooded Achilles himself
was coming up to them, with his retinue
of fierce Myrmidons, among them his commanders
Patroclus, Menésthius, Eudórus,
Pisánder, and Álcimus. It seemed to the men
that the ground shook at every step he took.
He seemed larger than a mere human being.
Such a handsome face, so magnificent,
such a beautiful body, so magnificent.   10
Their eyes opened wide and their tongues shrivelled.
Achilles was used to this demure silence.
It was the mighty cloud upon which he lived,

and from that cloud, the staring eyes of mortals
were as the stars above, numberless, unblinking.
He paid them no heed. The only noise in his life
was the thunder of war, which he relished.
And yet, in truth, what moves a cloud? Not a storm—
a storm expends a cloud. What moves a cloud,
however vast, is a soft wind not seen or felt   20
from below, and for Achilles that wind
was true, deep, and loyal friendship. And friendship
speaks gently. In his household, there was no shouting.
Away from the lung-spending tumult of war,
Achilles spoke and was spoken to gently,
nearly in a whisper. And so Achilles,
that god among men, strolled up to the men
and stopped among them—they who had never
been in such close neighbourhood to him but
had only seen him in the uproar of war.   30
He stopped among them and set his gaze upon

Psoas, who had just killed a slew of men
in a manner most bold and violent,
and said he to him, nearly in a whisper,
"And who are you, brave Argive? Whose son are you?
Where lies the land that raised you?" But Psoas
said nothing. He looked on and said nothing,
though a god among men was speaking to him.

Thersites spoke for him. "Lord Achilles,
this man here is the son of nobody.   40
His parents had no children, just as he
has no children, and his children—he has two—
will have no children, and none of them have parents,
not his children, their parents, or their grandparents,
and so on, into the sorry past and future,
generations of seedless orphans in the womb.
His is a long lineage of men with no yeast
and women with no dough, all of them bed-dead

their whole lives. As for me, I have six sons
and six daughters and I'm good to go for more.　　　　50
This floppy-eared mule only has his name,
Psoas, that much he has, an unusual name,
otherwise he has—and he is—nothing,
like me, whose name is Thersites, by the way.
Many Trojans have I killed these long years.
As for the land that raised him, it was Midea,
but not the great citadel, famed far and wide,
with a view as splendid as that from Olympus,
rather a rocky field lost in its shadow,
a prickly fuzz of brambles, some goats, nothing more.　　　　60
He is the son of nobody from nowhere,
like me. We have the same parents, we are brothers,
our children play together. By the way,
over there lies the man I just killed, mighty
Sandros of Lydia, son of Xanthelus,
a killer of many brave Argive men."

Again Lord Achilles spoke, in a whisper
as vast as the wind, his eyes steady on Psoas.
"You did well today, proud son of Midea.
You showed valour and determination. 70
We would do better if we had more men
like you in this war, men who spoke less and fought more.
I shall remember you, fearless Psoas."
God-blooded Achilles rested his hand upon
the son of nobody's shoulder and patted it.
Then he turned and walked away, his men in tow.

Psoas said nothing. Thersites looked around,
then, to no one in particular but loudly,
he said, "Well, well, I've just had a conversation
with no less than Achilles, that god among men, 80
son of Peleus and the sea nymph Thetis,
the greatest of our fighters, a demigod
whose fame and glory will live forever.

My deeds have attracted his attention.
You lost your tongue, didn't you, brave Psoas?"

Still, Psoas said nothing. The men around
stared at him. What man would not speak when spoken to
by the son of Peleus, that god among men?
But they dared not speak to the man who did not speak
to the man who always commanded speech since   90
he continued not to speak. They moved off.

"*He is the son of nobody from nowhere*" (61): I was left with nothing.

"*I shall remember you*" (73): I was left with nothing.

"*Then he turned and walked away*" (76): I was left with nothing.

"*Still, Psoas said nothing*" (86): I was left with nothing.

"*They moved off*" (91): Gail eventually picked up her phone and turned it back to the table in the emergency room. The machines were still beeping, but the doctors and nurses were standing in a circle around the table, silent and staring. You lay motionless.

The Funeral Pyre of Achilles

The greatest pyre-architects set to work.
They sent us off to the foothills of Mount Ida
to find pyre-wood worthy of a god,
oak, chestnut, pine, and fir, only the best.

Such a pyre we built for that god-blooded man!
It was a mountain, with a forest at its feet,
herds of sacrificial steeds, bulls, sheep, and swine,
an armoury of radiant battle gear,
a rich town's worth of goods and chattel, loot
given up by every man, poor and rich,   10
jars of fine oil, besides sculpted ivory,
a population of slain Trojan captives,
and the braided hair of the Myrmidons,

his people, who had all shorn their grieving heads.
Hovering above, like a swirl of clouds,
were countless fair-woven colourful vestments,
sprinkled with gleaming treasure, like stars in the night,
gold, silver, and bronze, precious gems, and amber, too.
At the very top of this mountain of wealth
rested a man, the most splendid of men.   20

The mountain went up in flames, a conflagration
of such brightness that it lit up the whole plain
and the nearby sea and the walls of Troy.
Atop those walls, looking like little puppets,
the people of Troy watched, as awestruck as we were.

The pyre burned for three days, sending billows of smoke
to all corners of the world, like messengers.
When it had burned itself out, there remained
a barrier of smouldering embers and bones,

much of it streaked with melted gold and silver, 30
or, where a gem had fallen, glaring up at us
like a bright eye peering from swarthy skin.
We quenched those embers with libational wine,
amphora after amphora, and with our tears.

Beyond this ring, at the very centre
of a vast carpet of pure soft white ash,
lay a single skeleton, gently nursed
by layer upon layer of flaming wood,
as if he had been rocked in the loving arms
of his mourning mother, the sea nymph Thetis. 40
Some say that through the roar of the flames they heard her
as she keened not over his mortality,
but over her abhorrent immortality.

We had never imagined such lovely bones,
so large, strong, and gleaming white, temple-like.

The skeleton of a god. We wept without cease
at the sight of them, not a man able
to stay on his feet or make himself understood
by his words. Truly, we were so sick at heart
we could not see how we could be men again,   50
but that is what we were, men, pitiful men.

"The greatest pyre-architects set to work" (1): What a sight this pyre must have been. Homer pulls off a similar stunt with the great pyre that cremates Patroclus, Achilles' beloved friend. Problem is, the Mycenaeans did not cremate, they buried, as any visitor to the Bronze Age beehive tombs of the Greek mainland will know. But a bonfire that reaches up to the sky, with a whole city of sacrificial victims, both human and animal, and a souk's worth of expensive offerings, makes for a far better scene than a dull inhumation in the ground.

I once heard firsthand of the appeal of sacred fire. At a dinner party at my parents' place one evening, I happened to mention Goa. In my restless days, I had travelled the length and breadth of India. An older, retired colleague of my mother's perked up.

"I was there, long ago," he said. This man did not give the impression of having lived a life of adventure, and yet, in the 1970s, he had travelled from Germany to India overland and he had spent time in Goa, where he had formed those deep, ephemeral friendships that travel produces. A whole group of them—there were Canadians, Americans, and Swedes, he recalled—lived on the beach as an impromptu collective, including a young man from somewhere in the American Midwest. Kansas? Nebraska? He couldn't remember. Nor could he remember his name. Possibly Kevin. At any rate, Kevin, who played the guitar, couldn't be found one night. Where has he gone? Hey, what's that on the water's edge? It was Kevin's body. He had drowned. A group of twenty-year-olds stood in a circle around his body, their first real encounter with death. What were they to do? Among his belongings they found an American phone number, but what were they to do with his body?

"Let's burn him," came the solemn suggestion from someone (with a deep voice?). Cremation was an Indian tradition, after all, and this was India. Everyone agreed, as if it were the obvious thing to do.

"So that's what we did," said the man, my mother's colleague. (You have to imagine the blinking consternation around the dinner table.) "India is a country of wood fires, so we gathered wood and built this huge pyre. Then we put Kevin's body on it, guitar, backpack, sleeping bag, everything we could find of his, and he burned all night. We chanted and kept adding wood. Then, in the morning, someone went into Panjim to call his parents."

In a farmhouse in Nebraska a rotary phone rang and rang, until a mother answered. Thetis then, Kevin's mother now.

Does it matter, this substituting of fire for burial? Can the real beehive tombs not stand right next to the fictional fires of Homer and Thersites? Such a laissez-faire attitude has the appeal of putting to one side the muffled communication of archaeology and the half-answers of history and leaves us to explore freely the infinite territory of literature, much like forgetting the unrewarding quest for the Jesus of history frees the believer to explore the more significant Jesus of faith. Cut the Trojan War's tenuous umbilical cord to history and the child can grow naturally.

"The greatest pyre-architects set to work" (1): Dear Helen, when we die and we come to drink from the river that makes us forget, know that I will not drink the drop that makes me forget you. And while I live, I shall not forget you in some other way.

"a population of slain Trojan captives" (12): "Mr. Harlow, do not think that your dereliction of duty will go unsanctioned! I'll make sure that Professor Gordon MacPherson is made aware of it."

"We wept without cease" (46): At Aulis, on the Greek mainland, Agamemnon waits for a favourable wind to carry his forces across the Aegean to Troy, but Artemis rebuffs him, day after day, angry that he killed a deer in a grove sacred to her. Seers tell the king that only if he sacrifices his eldest daughter, Iphigenia, will the goddess allow the winds to change. The king agrees and his daughter is lured from Mycenae, told that she is to marry Achilles. She is sacrificed, and the winds promptly turn. The Greek fleet sails out.

That, too, is a commonality between the story of Troy and the story of Jesus: the acquiescent sacrifice of an offspring without which neither story can proceed. In both, the future is begot by killing the future.

But how could Agamemnon go on? How could he put one foot before the other? How could he even breathe? Indeed, how could God go on?

"We wept without cease" (46): You died. While I was away in England, you were swept away by influenza in a matter of days. A not-feeling-well worsened until your mother, in a sudden panic, called an ambulance. The doctors did all they could—imagine, a child is in your hands and her vitals are failing—using every resource and tool they had, trying to pull off the miracle that is modern medicine. Your mother was there the whole time, in the emergency room, watching them, watching you, she saw it all, as did I, mostly. You were a little girl on an operating table, surrounded by frantic doctors and nurses. But they couldn't do it. You died, your lungs drowned. Gail called me from the hospital. I didn't answer at first. I didn't hear the phone. I was working. I was in the moment. You were just under the weather. Kids get sick all the time. You understand that, don't you?

"not a man able to stay on his feet or make himself understood by his words" (47–49): I stood outside the Ancient World Library. I looked around at the people around me, going about their regular business. What to do? Where to go?

Just then I saw Professor Cubitt, walking on the other side of the road. A man who had lost his son. He came level to the library, crossed over, and walked by me without noticing me, that habit of Oxford denizens of ignoring the milling crowds of tourists. He entered the Ancient World Library. A man on his way to work. A man and his archaeology.

"Truly, we were so sick at heart" (49): You died.

"men, pitiful men" (51): I was left with nothing.

Prince Mestor and the Son of Nobody Fight

Said Prince Mestor to the son of nobody,
"You should kill your own king, if you're so upset.
You're doing the bidding of a scheming liar.
It's Agamemnon who's to blame for your ills."

Replied the son of nobody to Prince Mestor,
"I don't care about my king or his lies.
Never has a king done me any good,
whether when speaking the truth or lying.
I came here not for my king but for myself,
not to win glory and honour, but loot."   10

"And how much loot do you have so far, Psoas?"

Replied Psoas, "None. Everything I've won
I've had to trade to stay alive. I have nothing."

Said Prince Mestor of Troy, "And what—I am *loot*?"
In a rage he threw his spear, but missed his target
as Psoas narrowly deflected it,
more luck than talent, the angle of his shield,
the side the spear was coming on. In response,
Psoas cast his spear, which Mestor flicked away
easily with his shield, all talent, no luck.   20

The prince marched forward, shield up, sword raised,
    eyes fixed
on the son of nobody, who stood his ground.
Down came Mestor's glinting blade on his shield,
cutting the hide and splintering the wood.
The prince raised his sword and did it once more,
cutting the hide and splintering the wood.

The prince raised his sword and did it a third time,
cutting the hide and splintering the wood.
The man behind the shield shook but did not falter,
but now there was nothing left of his shield.   30
He threw the useless straps off and said, "Come, come,"
to the prince, raising his sword, standing his ground.

Down came Mestor's glinting blade onto Psoas's.
The swords clashed loudly, and right away
the son of nobody's broke into three pieces.
He threw the useless hilt away, and said, "Come, come,"
to the prince, who laughed and replied, "Run, run."
But Psoas did not run. He stood his ground.

The prince growled, "Not three blows did your shield last,
not one your sword, yet you dare stand there, you dog?"   40
Mestor swung his sword and only by luck,
no talent, did Psoas manage to keep his head,

though not his helmet, which was struck and went flying.
The man under it shook but did not falter,
but now he had no weapons and little armour.

The son of nobody brought his hands down
and removed his greaves, which he tossed aside.
Next, without pause, he undid his wood plates,
front and back, dirty and torn, which he threw away.
His taslet, secondhand, and his tunic, besmirched,   50
lastly his sandals, worn, these too he flung off.
Before the prince now stood a naked man, who said,
"Come to one who is as naked as a dog, come."

Mestor was further angered by the impudence
and he attacked. This way and that his glinting blade
swung and thrust at the son of nobody.
But lo, now that he was unencumbered (and mad),
the man moved like the wind, turning, jumping,

ducking, dodging, evading every swing and thrust,
never shaking and never faltering.   60
He favoured the side of Mestor that held the shield,
hiding in front of it, turning as the prince turned,
making it his own defence. Round and round they spun,
until the prince, in a rage, threw the shield aside.
"What need do I have of a shield with you?"
shouted he to the son of nobody.

Now the prince attacked with his sword alone,
but lo, the man moved like the wind, turning, jumping,
ducking, dodging, evading every swing and thrust,
never shaking and never faltering,   70
until the prince, in a rage, threw his sword aside.
"What need do I have of a sword with you?"
shouted he to the son of nobody.

Now the prince attacked with his hands alone,

but lo, the man moved like the wind, slipping
from his every grip, yanking at his armour,
until the prince, in a rage, tore off his plates,
bronzed and burnished, his greaves, taslet, and tunic,
fine and clean, lastly his sandals, splendid,
until before Psoas stood a naked man.   80
"What need do I have of armour with you?"
shouted the prince to the son of nobody.
"Come to one who is as naked as the sun, come."

Prince Mestor of Troy and the son of nobody,
there, not far from the banks of the Scamander,
fought with their naked bodies and their bare hands.
They punched and they shoved, they grabbed and they twisted,
they fell and they rolled, they pinned and they shoved free,
they spat and they kicked, they shouted and they cursed.

In the end, it was just another mortal clash.   90

The son of nobody rose, while at his feet
one of the fifty sons of Priam lay dying,
one of the fifty suns of Troy went dark.

Psoas won, and he should have left it at that.
But the son of nobody's wrath knew no bounds.
In a rage, he stomped upon the dying man,
he caught up rocks and smashed them down on him,
he lifted him up and bit into his flesh—
but of the mutilations of the prince's corpse,
heinous and unsightly, I will say no more. 100

All the while the son of nobody shouted,
"No, you are not loot, Prince Mestor of Troy,
but you displeased me by insulting my wife,
whom I love just as much as you loved yours.
Not an hour goes by that I don't think of her,
not a day that I am happy in her absence.

Every day I miss the children we have made.
My heart has gone dark for not seeing them.
Much have I dwelt upon your unpleasant words.
This is what you get for uttering them, Mestor. 110
Lo! Who is that woman atop the walls,
the one shrieking and tearing her hair out?
Is that your wife? Look, my lady: all a mash!"

Psoas stood in a patch of soil whose wine colour
the sun and rain would soon enough wash away.

A fellow Argive ran up to him, breathless,
Chromatis of Tiryns, son of Olmander,
it was, who would live to see the end of the war.
Said he to him, "Psoas, hello? *Hello?*
I am speaking to you. You've lost your mind 120
with this foe. Who was he? And what were you thinking?
Any Trojan fighter could have picked you off.

What god was protecting you, rash fool—and why?
But who can tell, other than all-seeing seers,
what the gods want, or why they do what they do?"

Psoas said nothing, only swayed and staggered.
He made to pull away, without arms or shield,
naked but for a coat of blood and grime,
to return to his tent, a broken man,
the most broken man I have ever seen,   130
but behind him a man, unseen, cleared his throat
and said he in a deep voice to Psoas,
"You won, Psoas, and you should have left it at that."

"*Prince Mestor of Troy and the son of nobody . . . fought with their naked bodies and their bare hands*" (84, 86): The equality of the naked.

"*you displeased me by insulting my wife, whom I love just as much as you loved yours*" (103–104): It seems that the linchpin of *The Psoad*, the central cause of its main action, a commoner's assault on a prince, is neither class inequality nor wealth inequity, though these are most certainly motifs in the epic, but the offence taken by a husband at an insult hurled at his wife. What exactly did Prince Mestor say of Psoas's wife, whom he never met, had no basis to know even existed, just casually disparaged while fighting a war? I had to go back through all my work to find out. It was that she was "chicken-headed" (see *Prince Mestor and the Son of Nobody Meet for the First Time*, page 106, line 28). That is the throwaway insult Psoas dwells on for so long, the resentment building until he explodes. How very Ancient Greek. The love of uxor is not unique to *The Psoad*. The premise of *The Iliad* is that a wife has been taken away and her husband badly wants her back. *The Odyssey* is a slow-burning declaration of love and fidelity to a wife. Ten years it takes Odysseus, enduring every adversity, before he can return to his Penelope, and he is no more forgiving of the suitors' offences against his wife than Psoas is of Mestor's offence.

"*Psoas stood in a patch of soil whose wine colour the sun and rain would soon enough wash away*" (114–115): Was it that day? Or the next? I don't remember. "Put off the funeral," I said to Gail on another video call.

"Why?"

"I need to finish *The Psoad*. I'm nearly there."

"What? Are you kidding me?"

"No. There's nothing we can do about what happened. The fune—"

"I did everything I could!"

"I'm sure you did. But since you mention it, where were you at home when she was sick?"

"What do you mean? I was with her."

"All the time?"

"Yes. Well, I worked at the dining room table when she was sleeping. I was just downstairs. What are you saying? Are you saying I neglected Helen? It didn't look like it was anything serious. She was just a little sick. You would have done the same thing. Actually, you would have skipped off to the university."

"I'm just wondering if it would have made a difference if she got to the hospital earlier."

"You don't think I've thought that a million times? But no, it wouldn't have made a difference. I *asked*. By the time it looked serious, it was too late. The fluid in her lungs was too great. But so typical of you to lay it on me. I was maybe downstairs, but you were a million miles away in England."

"You don't think I've thought *that* a million times? I'm not accusing you of anything."

"Helen was dying, she was *dying*, and they couldn't do anything to save her. They tried pumping out her lungs, they zapped her chest, they did everything they could. It was happening right in front of my eyes. It was awful, it was unspeakably awful. You have no idea."

"Actually, I do, Gail. I do. It all came through that little screen. We've lost—"

I stopped. The words stopped me. Gail and I stared at each other for a moment, the pain hovering between us, both our phones shaking in our hands. I managed to continue.

"We've lost our precious girl. She's gone. I have to live with that, as do you. And like Agamemnon after Aulis, I'm—"

"Oh spare me the classical references! I don't want to hear about goddamn Agamemnon."

"I'm just asking that we delay the funeral. There's no rush to bury her. We waited over a year and a half to bury my dad's ashes. I'm—"

"We're not talking about your dad here. You're one flight away. Fly in, fly out."

"Two flights away, actually. I don't want to. The Oxyrhynchus Papyri are here, at Oxford, not in Canada."

And I—we—could not afford it.

"WHO CARES ABOUT YOUR WORK! Your daughter dies and you don't want to come home? *What is wrong with you?* You have a heart of stone."

"No I don't. This is something I'm doing for Helen. It's helping me heal."

"And what do I have to help me heal, Harlow? What do *I* have?"

"You had the gift of the last nine months of her life."

"Come home."

"Home? May I remind you of the last words you said to me at the airport, whispered in my ear? And how many times did you call me while I was away?"

"You're unbelievable. There never was a grudge you didn't love."

"You're one to talk."

"Okay, you win. YOU WIN! We'll delay the funeral."

"Thank you."

"And your daughter, by the way, wouldn't give a fuck about your stupid Greek epic."

Gail hung up.

You died, and I did not return home. I stayed at Oxford to finish *The Psoad*. I took advantage of the favourable winds and sailed from Aulis, my ship's sails so many tatters of papyrus, my destination a gleaming citadel, leaving behind a daughter who had died and her distraught mother. I spent every waking hour in the Papyrology Work Room. That is to say, like Agamemnon, like God, I got back to work.

    Helen, is that true? Would you not care about the struggles of an ordinary man long ago?

Hades Speaks to Psoas

A man cleared his throat and said he in a deep voice,
"You won, Psoas, and you should have left it at that."

It was Hades, Lord of the Underworld.
Psoas had meant to return to his tent,
but instead he was hoisted up in the air,
the dark lord holding him tightly by the scrotum,
his fist a hard ball and his knuckles white.
Trembling and gasping, the son of nobody said,
"My lord, I did not expect to meet you today."

Replied Hades, "What everyone tells me.   10
It's a rare mortal who meets in the flesh
Zeus, Poseidon, Hera, Athena, Apollo,

or any other of my fellow immortals.
But every mortal meets me and comes to my home.
It is announced by the progress of every day,
dawn to dusk, by the passage of every season,
spring to winter, by the slacking of skin
and the greying of hair and the stooping of back,
year after year. Every candle burns out, yet
the surprise on the faces of mortals, 20
the shock in their eyes, the disbelief in their minds
when the fated happens is like the look
of a child the first time it sees the sea.
All mortals come to me the same, equal.
If they die equal, why should they not live equal?
It was a good line I gave you, wasn't it?
'I am no less of a man than you are.'
I was watching you, wondering what you'd do.
It was I who gave you the rock—see, that one—
with which you struck Mestor's forehead and killed him. 30

But look what you've done, Psoas, the mess.
You won and you should have left it at that."

Asked Psoas, "Is today my last day on earth?"

Replied Hades, "As it happens, no, it is not.
I don't see the Fates coming to fetch you.
I'm out for a stroll. A little sunshine
and fresh air. Persephone, my darling wife,
is away for the season and I miss her.
I thought I'd come to see this noisy tiff
that has so taken my brothers and sisters.   40
It has it all, they tell me. Where have you been?
It's all they talk about, my brothers and sisters,
about Argives and Trojans, Trojans and Argives.
They take sides and every day toss the dice,
then watch what happens and argue about it.
Have they nothing better to do? I have a job.

I'm the one who gets the most business out of this.
There are days when the brook behind my home,
the Styx, is clogged with ships poor Charon has to guide.
Yet I've never visited. So here I am." 50

Asked Psoas, "So today I live on and die not?"

Replied Hades, "Enough already. Are you deaf?
You will live. Ask again and I will hurt you.
So that over there, of course, is sacred Troy.
Nice walls. Those gracefully tailored soldiers
are the Trojans, fighting for their women
and children, for everything they hold precious.
And here we have the grubby, lice-ridden
Argives in their thousands. Your crappy ships are there.
But fill in the details. Be my narrator. 60
Over there, who is that man with the pig's face?"

Replied Psoas, "It is Lord Agamemnon."

"The fat one next to him with the bulging eyes?"

Replied Psoas, "It is Lord Menelaus."

"Rat-face over there, peeing behind his shield?"

Replied Psoas, "It is Lord Odysseus."

"The beefy ones with the eyes too close together?"

Replied Psoas, "Diomédes and Ajax."

"That old one, trying to get it hard with the slave boy?"

Replied Psoas, "It is wise Lord Nestor." 70

"And upon the walls of Troy, who are they?"

Replied Psoas, "I don't know, Lord Hades.
They are too far for my weak eyes to see."

"See this drop of water? Look through it. And now?"

Replied Psoas, "Now I see those upon the walls."

"So many women atop. Yet among them,
Helen of Troy shines incomparably.
She reminds me of my Persephone.
That is the chameleon trick of great beauty,
that it glows with individual colour   80
to every set of eyes. And next to Helen,
that sad old man, leaning upon his staff?"

Replied Psoas, "It is Priam, great king of Troy."

"The beautiful and the weary, side by side.
Now I can see why this tale has so beguiled
my brothers and sisters. And this one at my feet,
whom you've so butchered, once a mosaic,
the likeness whole and clear, now scattered tesserae,
Prince Mestor of Troy, son of King Priam
and Queen Hecuba, brother of Hector,   90
Paris, and forty-seven other brothers,
besides many sisters. A delightful child
he was, always a smile upon his face,
full of tricks, yet kind-hearted and fair-minded.
He grew up to be a good husband, father,
and soldier, devoted to all. Look at him now."

Said Psoas, "I was angry at him, Lord Hades."

"Life is a delicate invention of the heart.
Why wreck it? Why can't we all just get along?

You won and you should have left it at that.   100
I tire of anger. There is no anger
in my kingdom. I rule it sternly but justly,
with a level voice and an even temper.
Contrary to what some mortals might think,
mine is a peaceable realm. Every mortal
who crosses the Styx exchanges his or her
lot of anger for ten times the lot of sorrow,
every good measure pressed down, shaken together,
running over. You hear groans, cries, and weeping
in my sombre inn, but you don't hear anger.   110
In my household, there is no shouting.
Compare that to my brother Poseidon's waters.
They're always noisy and nothing is ever still.
Winds blow, waves lap, currents disturb, and what about
storms? No such wrathful weather where I live.
As for Zeus, he lives in the same room as you lot,
and, well, look around—is this a quiet room?

Have you ever seen so many vexed people
wreaking such havoc and making such a racket?
No, there is no anger in my kingdom, only   120
quiet stress, deep regret, and measureless sadness.
I am wonderfully hospitable—
why does no one ever say that of me?
I turn no one back who knocks at my door.
Room and board are always available.
And I get along so nicely with my queen.
Why has no one ever taken note of that?
We never trade in sharp words or hold grudges.
There's none of that spatting and whoring-about
to which my brothers and sisters so ardently   130
stoop. How can they bear being so endlessly upset?
My Persy and I are truly devoted
to each other, with sweetness and faithfulness.
I miss her terribly when she's not around,
so I go for long, calisthenic walks.

Do you know what I do while on my rambles?"

Replied Psoas, "I do not, Lord Hades."

"Take heed of this advice, mortal Psoas,
as it comes from a god. Do as I do
and you will avoid meeting me too soon. 140
While on my jaunts I may do the following:
I'll sprint a thousand leagues as fast as I can,
faster than Hermes. Nary taking a break,
I'll grip the edge of lofty Mount Olympus,
feet dangling in the clouds, and I'll pull myself up
until my chin reaches past the summit,
drop down, and do this a thousand times, nonstop.
Next, I'll lie flat on the ground and push myself off
until my arms are fully extended,
keeping my body as straight as a plank, 150
then I'll lower myself and do it again

until I've reached a count of two thousand.
Right after, I will stand tall, then squat low,
hips below the knees, then stand once more, only that,
but three thousand times. I'm not done. After that,
I'll sprint another thousand leagues. Then I'm done.

"Or I'll do this: from my brother Poseidon,
I'll borrow a thousand ships and row them
a thousand times around Oceanus,
after which I'll take hold of a good-sized rock— 160
what you feeble mortals call a mountain range—
and, keeping my back straight, heave it to my chest.
I'll squat, then stand and hoist this hulking mass
high into the clouds, my arms straight. I'll squat down
and repeat, until I've counted to five thousand.
Then I'll do three thousand Olympian pull-ups.

"I do something like this every day, with brio,

never the same, always hard, and each time,
at the end of it, I collapse, nearly senseless,
my heart pounding like the mightiest earthquake,   170
my lungs heaving like the fiercest storm at sea,
and sweat running off my body more freely
than all the waters of the rivers on earth.
That is what I do while on my rambles,
when I am not thinking about my sweetheart,
or observing the foolish doings of mortals."

Asked Psoas, who trembled still before the dark lord,
"And what is the purpose of these great exertions,
Lord Hades, Master of the Underworld?"

Replied Hades, "It gives my immortality   180
a nice buff. My body, after spending
so much, finds itself with even more to spend.
And my mind is refreshed, having taken a rest

---

from its driven ways. I return to running
the Underworld with peace of mind and sharp purpose.
Of course, we have our issues, who doesn't?
There's my mother-in-law, speaking of anger.
Persy has a bit of a mother fixation,
and mother dear doesn't think much of my kin.
She finds them noisy, devious, and uncouth.   190
But we deal with our problems with an open heart,
truly seeking to understand each other.
I get to spend only half the year, that's it,
with my beloved. The rest of the year
I work in celibate solitude, with only
Cerberus for company, sweet dog that he is.
But I feel no anger, only acceptance.

"Oh look, over there, Achilles has returned.
His exploits have reached even my distant ears.
Look at him hack away at his enemies.   200

Achilles will have his glory and honour,
too right, that shiny *kleos* and *timē*
he so badly wants. Isn't that the trade-off
of being mortal, the chance to win fame
everlasting? Whereas god that I am,
what extra can I earn? Can I top up
the full cup of my immortal plenty?
Curious—a man is mortal and he aspires
to be immortal. He wants what he does not have.
Common enough. But is the converse true? 210
Do *I* want to be mortal? What a thought,
a god giving up on the bounty of life.
What could be so flavourful about death?
I'll talk to Persy about this. She's clever.
But she's not here at the moment. Perhaps
you can help. Dishing it out as you do,
and fearing it, you must know about death.
I don't. I am the tree, forever standing,

and you are the olive. Tell me, what flavour
does the oil of death have? Teach me about death." 220

So spoke Lord Hades in a deep, brilliant mumble
as he mashed the son of nobody's scrotum.
Psoas's skin crawled and his body trembled,
his teeth clattered and much did he groan, poor mortal.

Replied Psoas, "Teach you about death, my lord?"

Replied Hades, "Yes, teach me about death."

Said Psoas, "You are Master of the Underworld,
my lord. Is death not your daily business?"

Replied Hades, giving Psoas an extra squeeze,
"I know who I am, son of nobody. 230
I know the husk of death. You will bring me its flesh."

Psoas's skin crawled and his body trembled,
his teeth clattered and much did he groan, poor mortal.

Said Hades, "You will come to me, Psoas."

Gasped Psoas, "You said today I would not die."

Said Hades to the son of nobody,
"Who said anything about you dying?"

The Lord of the Underworld released the man
and the air exploded with battle noise.
Psoas stood in a patch of soil whose wine colour   240
the sun and rain would soon enough wash away.
(No one else among the men had seen Hades,
wearing as he was the gift from the Cyclops,
his helmet of invisibility.)

A fellow Argive came up to him, breathless,
Chromatis of Tiryns, son of Olmander,
it was, who would live to see the end of the war.
Said he to him, "Psoas, hello? *Hello?*
I am speaking to you. You've lost your mind
with this foe. Who was he? And what were you thinking?   250
Any Trojan fighter could have picked you off.
What god was protecting you, rash fool—and why?
But who can tell, other than all-seeing seers,
what the gods want, or why they do what they do?"

Psoas said nothing, only swayed and staggered.
He pulled away, with neither arms nor shield,
naked but for a coat of blood and grime,
to return to his tent, a broken man,
the most broken man I have ever seen.

"*the dark lord holding him tightly by the scrotum*" (6): Nine weeks later, the term was over, and so too was my scholarship. I flew back to Canada. As I travelled, my heart emptied out like a sack of wheat that has torn and, unseen, slowly depletes in a trickle of grain.

"*Persephone, my darling wife, is away for the season and I miss her*" (37–38): Mestor, Psoas, and now Hades—they all dearly love their wives. It's a sweet motif, this strand of uxoriousness in *The Psoad*, this praise of the happy wife who makes her husband happy. Homer, too, sings of this form of love, and of others: the love of men for their homeland, the love of brothers-in-arms, the love of mothers and fathers for their children, the love of children for their parents. *The Iliad* famously starts with the word "wrath" (μῆνιν—*mēnin*) and there is indeed a lot of wrath in the epic, expressed both in choleric language and grotesque brutality. Yet underlying this violence is love. It's interesting to compare the shape of *The Iliad* with that of the other foundational book of Western culture, the Gospels. With the Greek epic, we have men at war in the foreground, shouting and killing each other, and only in the background, in conversations on the side, do we hear men and women mourning their broken souls, while with the story of Jesus of Nazareth, we have love constantly discussed and concretely enacted in the foreground before a background of hatred and violence. It's the exact inverse of *The Iliad*.

"Persephone, my darling wife, is away for the season and I miss her" (37–38): Gail was at the airport. She hadn't offered to pick me up, I hadn't asked, but there she was. The glazed glass doors slid apart, revealing a throng of expectant people eyeing the travellers who were arriving. How powerful recognition is, its effect on the mind! She was standing there, gaze fixed on me. Her eyes. The set of her face. Medusa, snake-hair writhing and hissing, couldn't have frozen me more.

I had no fight in me. I saw Gail, but what I saw most was the empty space next to her.

"That is the chameleon trick of great beauty" (79): The lizard is truly a Psoadic obsession.

"mine is a peaceable realm" (105): We barely spoke. But what we did say—greetings, comments on the flight and the weather—came out gently. I looked out the window of the car, aware of the silence from the back seat. I was exhausted. I had caught a cheap flight, at the cost of spending a night at a transit airport, trying to sleep on chairs not meant to be beds. What amazes

now, when I think of it, is how we said not a word about you. Or rather, our silence said everything.

"for ten times the lot of sorrow, every good measure pressed down, shaken together, running over" (107–109): Yet again, phrasing that would find a Christian echo—more: an exact replication. From Luke 6:38:

> Give, and it will be given to you. A good measure, pressed down, shaken together, running over, will be put into your lap; for the measure you give will be the measure you get back.

Or is this mere coincidence, a false correlation, just the way ancient traders, both Trojan and Jewish, spoke of bushels, whether of grain, gifts, or, in this case, sorrow?

"That is what I do while on my rambles" (174): With Hades' workouts, we have here a mythical precursor of the later Greek celebration of athleticism, best exemplified by the original Olympics.

"Oh look, over there, Achilles has returned" (198): Except that Achilles is supposed to be dead by now. Could Thersites the bard have forgotten? What an irritating mistake. Or perhaps Hades is seeing what he wants to see, a god

rewinding the movie to look once more at a fine piece of action. Memory is like that, always available.

"a deep, brilliant mumble" (221): It is not clear to me how indistinct speech can be brilliant, but those are the words in the original. The bard must have had some image in his mind, a Marlon Brando of the ancient world, that didn't quite make it into his words. No matter. What we have here is a tearing aside of the surface humdrum and a raw gawk at ultimate reality.

Epiphanies were commonly accepted in antiquity. They were rarely as full-on as Psoas's encounter with Hades. Take this example, from Homer, after the two Ajaxes are revived by stirring words delivered by the prophet Calchas. Says one Ajax to the other:

> "Ajax, that must have been an immortal who left us,
> an Olympian, who was taking the form of Calchas,
> not the real man. I could tell from the way his feet moved
> as I watched from behind; it is easy to know a god.
> My heart has been struck by a jolt of courage, I feel
> my body tingling all over, my arms and legs
> surge with strength, and I long to go into battle." (13.68–75)

The way his feet moved? To the receptive Ancient Greek, what counted was not the form a god took, but the wondrous effect that resulted. An epiphany, therefore, was not usually a matter of seeing the actual face of a god but of detecting the mask that god might be wearing. A shower of meteors; a flight of birds; the tickle and tug of a dream; a stranger with striking features; thunder and winds; an oddly shaped potato; a loud sneeze; or a man shuffling his feet—all these might be a god speaking.

Well, no mask in this fragment. Hades cuts a lonely figure at Troy. *The Iliad* is a madly gregarious epic, in heaven as it is on earth, with the exception of Hades. While his Olympian brothers and sisters interact incessantly with each other and with mortals during the war, talking, shouting, pleading, arguing, threatening, attacking, protecting, deceiving, revealing, fleeing, returning, he makes only a single appearance in Homer's epic, and it is a late and brief one: in Book 20, he lets out a scream when the battles above ground are so tumultuous that he fears they will disrupt his kingdom. A scream, that's it. In *The Psoad*, he is no more sociable. He talks to no one, neither god nor human, except Psoas, and the encounter starts with Hades clearing his throat. Who clears their throat but someone who has not spoken for a while, or is shy, not used to company?

For the Greeks of old, death was not an embodied force. Hades did not live with death the way Poseidon inhabited the seas, or Zeus visited the earth.

Death was not something; it was nothing, it was the cessation and absence of life, it was a stoppage. Hence why Hades, the place, was so murky and unclear to the ancient imagination, more mood than landscape. Hence why Hades, the god, was notably unworshipped, because why worship a god who has nothing to offer? Hence why Hades, with that perfect Ancient Greek sense of contrast, should fall in love with, and remain ever faithful to, the daughter of the goddess of the harvest and fertility, yet, in the original traditions, have no children, because nothing is necessarily sterile.

Hades, in this sense, of absence, seems a very modern, irreligious embodiment of death. But it would be more accurate to say that it was pre-religious. In *The Odyssey*, when Odysseus travels to the Underworld, it is the abode not only of the likes of Tantalus and Sisyphus, but also of Achilles, Ajax, Tiresias. It is the place to which all the dead go, the bad *and* the good. At best, the good get to go to the greyish Elysian Fields, which were nothing like later conceptions of paradise. It would be close to a thousand years before poets like Virgil constructed an elaborate geography of Hades and transformed it into a moral landscape to which only the evil were banished. The next step was to have it be ruled by the active incarnation of evil, Satan, who was given colour, character, and baneful intent.

Being such a dispiriting, inevitable final destination, it makes sense that the weary Lord of Nothing, if stirred, would mourn the loss of anything and everything, because anything and everything is better than nothing. Already, when you have only a few minutes to live, you take this man's life, create a widow and orphans, fool that you are, and now this, this butchery of a good man's body? It's a lovely line from Hades: "Life is a delicate invention of the heart" (98).

For all his cool control and self-effacing probity, beyond his deep reserve, Hades is a pained god, the most of any Greek god, hence his grave temperament, hence why in *The Iliad* his only expression is a scream, hence why in *The Psoad* he misses so much the comfort of his wife. Even his maniacal exercise regime might be seen as an attempt to deal with the stress of moral pain.

Eventually, Hades would travel east. He is mentioned several times in the New Testament, even from the lips of Jesus: "And I tell you, you are Peter, and on this rock I will build my church, and the gates of Hades will not prevail against it" (Matthew 16:18). Left behind were his Olympian brothers and sisters, too life-intoxicated to understand the god-man from Nazareth. Death-soaked Hades is the only god to emigrate from the Hellenic cosmos to the Christian.

One is left wondering about the want expressed by Hades:

"I know the husk of death. You will bring me its flesh." (231)

The husk of death is clearly a reference to the lifeless corpse. It might also encompass the dismal disembodied mourning spirits that wander about Hades. But what is the flesh of death? What exactly does Hades want from Psoas?

"to return to his tent, a broken man, the most broken man I have ever seen" (258–259): My darling daughter, you were supposed to be Helen of Troy, celebrated, if fought over, not Iphigenia of Mycenae, sacrificed.

I say it again: how could Agamemnon go on? How could he put one foot before the other? How could he even breathe?

The Trojan Goat

It was Epéüs, the master carpenter,
son of Panópeus, good with his fists
and good with wood, who had the idea,
noting as he did a fatal weakness
in the great wooden portals of the Scaean Gate
and devising an astute way to exploit it,
until the King of Ithaca made it his own,
clever then, clever now, clever always,
but theft is a king's right. So it was done.

We left a pure white goat before the Scaean Gate.   10
We tethered the animal to a gold stake,
decked it with garlands of fragrant flowers,
circled it with candles that shone in the night—

---

a gift to the gods who had not favoured us,
a bitter admission of defeat to our foes
(a baited hook, the menace hidden deep).
Then we left that cursed shore, clearing out our camp,
taking everything with us, leaving poorer,
lesser, and fewer than when we had arrived,
departing at night so that the Trojans   20
might not pursue us, our orders whispered
mouth to ear rather than roared in the air.
We had come as lions. We left as mice.

We sailed to Tenedos, which we had secured.
We moored our ships on the opposite side,
the sails down, our men ashore under curfew
day and night, no fires or shouting allowed
under penalty of death, while we waited.
Our scouts were told to report only one thing:
the sound of music and the singing of drunks.   30

In the meantime, we covered our prows with pitch
and we dyed our sails with the darkest berries.
Our blacksmiths, following the careful instructions
of Odysseus, had devised four heavy hooks,
the eyes so large a man's fist fit easily,
but the points quite flat. Even the blacksmiths
did not know what they were for. We waited.

It took the Trojans eight days truly to believe
their good fortune. On the morning of the ninth,
they began to celebrate. By evening   40
the city was a feast, our scouts reported.
Celebratory fires were alight everywhere,
trumpets were blaring, drums were beating, and
song was coming from all corners of the city.

Two ships slipped out with fifty brave men aboard,
fifty men perched between victory and death.

They were Neoptolemus, Menelaus,
Odysseus, Sthenelus, Diomédes,
Philoctétes, Menestheus, Anticlus,
Thoas, Polypoetes, Ajax the Smaller,   50
Eurypylus, Thrasymede, Meriones,
Idómeneus, Podaleirius,
Eurymachus, Teucer, Ialmenus,
Thalpius, Antimachus, Leonteus,
Eumelus, Euryalus, Amphimachus,
Demophöon, Agapenor, Akamas,
Meges, Epéüs, Psoas—and then I,
next to my friend—besides Agamemnon,
and yet more fearless Argives, to fifty.
This very day, our commanders whispered,   60
either we will sleep in Troy, or in Hades.
We brought only what we needed for our last fight,
no tents, little food, nothing to sleep a night.

Two ships more slipped out with the four large gifts
of King Memnon of Aethiopia,
one of sacred Troy's last but greatest allies.
Achilles, in the days before he died,
had killed him in a hard-fought battle, after which
Memnon's soldiers had lost heart and returned home.
But these they had left behind, with their attendants.   70

Then slipped out the rest of our ragged fleet.
Years ago, we had come to Troy as bright as day,
our ships and our hearts. Now, as black as night,
we returned to Troy, our ships and our hearts.

We forward four rowed, to invite no reflection
from the night sky off our sails, and we rowed
in utter silence, each man dipping his oar
with utmost caution. The rest of our fleet
hid in the waters of Trojan Bay, awaiting
our signal, should we succeed in our mission.   80

When our ships reached the shores of the city,
we unloaded and covered the gifts with our sails
to make them darker still, and we marched behind them,
unseen. What did the drunk guards of Troy think they saw?

At the Scaean Gate, we removed the sails
from their backs, rolled them up, and threaded them
through the eyes of the four hooks. Odysseus
looked nervous as he directed the men,
but the master carpenter's scheme went as planned.
They worked the points of the hooks deep into the gap   90
between the great wooden portals of the gate,
and then those giant creatures, gifts of Hera,
wrapped their freakish noses around the rolled-up sails
and tore the Scaean Gate off its hinges.

We poured into Troy like a river of lava.

"*It was Epéüs ... who had the idea*" (1, 3): This is the second reference to Epéüs in *The Psoad*. In an earlier fragment (see *The Arrival: The Porcupine's Back*, pages 48–49, lines 85–94), concerning Psoas's idea to deal with the sharp stakes hidden in the harbour waters off the coast of the Troad that are costing the Greeks so many ships, Thersites the bard mentions Epéüs in passing:

> It was Psoas, the son of nobody,
> who said it first. I was there, I heard him.
> Lakander, a potter from Dendra, heard him, too,
> and hollered it: "RUN A SHIP ALONG THE SHORELINE!"
> Another, on a near ship, understood at once.
> Odysseus, King of Ithaca, it was,
> clever then, clever now, clever always.
> He said it even louder and gave orders,
> making the idea his own, but theft
> is a king's right. (Talk to Epéüs about that.)

So this is the idea stolen by Odysseus, not the Trojan Horse but the Trojan Hook. Once again in *The Psoad*, Thersites the bard remembers and celebrates a clever commoner over a scheming noble.

"with the four large gifts of King Memnon of Aethiopia" (64–65): This is an astonishing twist on the Trojan Horse. But *The Psoad* has credibility on its side. In practical terms, which is more believable: the idea of Bronze Age Greeks constructing a portable, structurally sound, physically accurate, two-story wooden horse in which fifty men can hide, and the wily, war-hardened Trojans being so stupid as to fall for the ruse and dragging the big thing into their city—or the natural strength of elephants?

To sift possibility and plausibility serves no purpose. If there ever was a full-out Trojan War featuring the Greeks, and if the Greeks actually won it by getting past the walls of Troy, we will never know how they did it (though there are elephants in Ethiopia, a known ally of the Trojans, and the Greeks knew about elephants, since they traded in ivory. And once, in the south of India, I saw with my own eyes the power of an elephant. A flatbed truck had driven off the road. The gradient was steep, the

truck large, yet the elephant, taking hold of a thick rope that had been tied to the back of the truck, heaved it back onto the road in great, powerful jerks. It was an astonishing display of brute strength. And this was an Indian elephant, smaller and less brawny than an African). We're talking myth here.

What is more interesting to contemplate is why one image survived with such clarity, while the other disappeared entirely but for this one fragment. Why did the Trojan Elephants have so little resonance? This is all the more surprising if one looks a little later in history. Elephants pop up. Most notably, there was Hannibal, who in the third century BCE marched across Europe to Rome with elephants, but others used them for military purposes, too, Julius Caesar among them. Psoas's elephants are surely the precursors of these later elephants.

The answer perhaps lies in the physicality of the animals. The Greeks have been fighting for ten years for nothing except the near complete breakdown of the human spirit. They are weak and helpless. When they contrive an improbable win, it is only as a result of the help of absurd-looking animals left behind by a barbarian enemy. What triumph is there in that? It makes Agamemnon *feel* like an elephant, with a long nose and floppy ears. It won't do. Better to make it a fake animal, whose real strength—men, *us!*—will pour out of its belly. Why not a horse, the animal for which the Trojans were so famed? There, now the puny Greek warrior can stand tall and strong. And with that, a piteous goat is transformed into a magnificent example of human ingenuity, a wooden horse, and into its shadow are cast the Trojan Elephants.

If the reader will recall these lines from earlier in the epic (see *The Role of Horses*, page 129, lines 24–27):

> Soon this was a war fought with no horses—
> don't let any other bard tell you otherwise.
> Kings and commoners, we all walked into battle,
> though it pleased the angry kings not at all.

After eliminating the horse in its physical incarnation, Thersites the bard now eliminates it even as a metaphor, substituting a goat as the Greeks' gift to the Trojans. What a humbler, humbling offering, even when tethered to a gold stake (11).

Is Thersites' distaste for the horse not similar to Jesus's? Both the Trojans and the Romans flaunted the animal as a symbol of their superiority. And if you object to the symbolic Trojan horse, will you not also object to the symbolic Trojan man who owns it, Prince Mestor?

If that is the explanation for the absence of the horse in the epic and of Psoas's assault upon a prince, then Thersites' *Psoad* is the precursor of a spirit that would blossom later, both in Greece, with the rise of the idea of citizenship, and in Palestine, with Jesus. And it also explains the prominent role given to Hades, a god who, like Jesus, mingled with all, no matter their class. That, then, would be the specificity of *The Psoad*, and the possible explanation for its damnation and near disappearance: its condemnation of unfair privilege and its radical call for egalitarianism. Such a call would rankle the ruling elites of any time, Thersites' as well as ours. The excess of the few impoverishes the many. Our city of treasure and trust lies in ruins.

"Years ago, we had come to Troy as bright as day, our ships and our hearts. Now, as black as night, we returned to Troy, our ships and our hearts" (72–74): At the wheel, Gail took a wrong turn, which she didn't correct when she could.

"Where are we going?" I asked.

"You'll see soon enough."

Should I have apologized then for making her wait, for making you wait? Was the delay worth it? I should have said I was sorry, but at that moment the only thing I wanted was to die and I could barely speak. Would that Gail had crashed the car.

The Sacking of Troy

War was back. War was running through the streets.
War was entering every house. *Hello! Hello!*

After years of living in tents and ships,
it was a wondrous sight to see the streets of Troy.
They were entirely paved, and they ran next
to marble sidewalks fringed by neat houses
and shops, by imposing temples and palaces.
Beautiful plazas were decorated
with trees held hostage within stone circles.
What a pleasure to see nature held prisoner.   10

Such empty riches we found behind every door.
Pottery workshops with dozens of wheels.

Smithies with forges that once burned like volcanoes.
Smelting and casting workshops where rich ores
had been refined to an exquisite degree.
Other workshops where artisans had plied
their extravagant skills upon precious stones
or exotic woods. Dye-works with numberless vats.
Stables fit not for an Argive king's horses,
but for the king himself, so splendid were they.   20
Hearths so vast several sheep could be roasted
upon them, besides many tripods kept hot,
with giant chimneys. Everything from everywhere
was here. This city was the centre of the world.
Sacred Ilios did not just make and trade
gold, gems, and fine fabrics, sacred Ilios
was itself gilded, gemmed, and finely clothed.
But there wasn't much food to be found, was there?

War was back. War was running through the streets.

War was entering every house. *Hello! Hello!*   30

Amidst the dearth we found pockets of wealth.
Ostrich eggs, ornaments of alabaster,
vials of sweet perfume. Men grasped at everything,
like starving beggars, Argive fighting Argive.
The result was predictable, was it not?
Broken eggs, wrecked ornaments, shattered vials.

How is it that soldiers conquering a city,
striding in like mighty victors, turned so quickly
to slaves moving the chattels of a rich man?
But so it was. Argives, while killing their foes,   40
yelled, shoved, and threw fists over every last spoil,
beds, chairs, tables, even stools. Yes, even stools.
Each man, of his pile of loot, cried in a rage,
"Mine! Mine! Mine!" For nothing. It all vanished.

We killed royals, nobles, priests, commoners, slaves.
Men, women, children. In streets, in homes, in temples.
Everyone, everywhere. *Hello! Hello!*
We slaughtered people who had no warcraft—
they grabbed the swords that were about to kill them.
On the ground, all round, so many fingers. 50

Many were killed half-asleep, barely aware
of what was going on. Many were killed
mid-rush, attempting some form of defence.
Many were killed as they fled, their backs exposed.

War was back. War was running through the streets.
War was entering every house. *Hello! Hello!*

We started fires that raced ahead of us,
doing our work of destruction, and flushing out
hidden foes. But care had to be taken.

Fire helped us, then asked loudly to be paid,
and its wage was exorbitant. Many Argives,
mad with the thirst for revenge, were burned alive
as the thirsty fire arrived hot on their heels.
Up in flames with the Trojans—good riddance—
went much of war's reward, our hard-won plunder,
every last stool. And what is a victory
if you have nothing to bring home but word of it?
If we had truly insisted on plunder,
we would have brought back grey ashes and black soot.

Framed by a doorway: a woman in the dark,
alight like a torch, a staggering skeleton,
clutching to her bosom a child, also
burning brightly, both of them crying out.

For ten years we were curious about the view
from the walls of Troy. Well, it was a fine view.

And what better place to exterminate
the seed and lineage of those we hated?
Over the parapet they flew, wide-eyed,
wailing and grappling, a rain of children.

War was back. War was running through the streets. 80
War was entering every house. *Hello! Hello!*

Some Trojans survived, escaping through gates
they threw open after keeping them closed so long.
But if Troy were a man, then only his mouth
got away, that small part of the body,
just big enough to tell—lips trembling and
teeth chattering—of the fiery destruction
of his city at our hands, the greatest
conflagration the world has ever known.
It was only the mouth that got away— 90
all else of the body of Troy we destroyed.

I heard a voice above the roaring din.
"Who is that figure behind Menelaus?
Yes, it is she! Besmirched though she is with soot,
dishevelled and terrified, her eyes cast down
like a slave girl's, who would shine with such beauty
if not the coveted object of our long war.
It is Queen Helen herself. Great Zeus, look at her!
Her face, the perfection of its proportions.
How she moves, the grace of her every part.   100
I do feel a thunderbolt has rent my heart!
Will she be happy, back with her first husband?
Was she ever happy with Prince Paris?
Or did this terrible war wreck it all for her?"

"*War was back. War was running through the streets. War was entering every house.* **Hello! Hello!**" (1–2): We turned into the parking lot of a funeral home, one we'd been to a few times over the years. It was ten thirty in the morning, on a weekday.

Had she arranged the funeral to be just then, upon my arrival? But the parking lot was empty. And when we entered the lobby, there was no one except for a man dressed in a black suit. The label on his lapel said his name was Bryan. Fifties, portly, sober. He greeted us. He seemed uncomfortable.

What, a funeral for two people? But when I glanced into the room where the ceremonies were held, by all appearances a church—pews, lectern, stained glass—but without any of the usual symbols, no crosses, the stained glass just panes of colour, telling no stories, a secular space imitating a religious one, it too was empty. No wreath, no coffin.

The man, Bryan, directed us to a set of stairs that went down.

We went down, not a word spoken.

A hallway. Some doors. One that he opened.

"In here," he said quietly.

"*War was back. War was running through the streets. War was entering every house.* **Hello! Hello!**" (29–30): It was the funeral home's morgue. Or mortuary, as Bryan gently corrected me, perhaps thinking the word would change how the room felt and that I would be soothed. A drab, neon-lit room, the air temperature somewhat cool, though perhaps that was my imagination. I noticed there wasn't a single personal touch; no artwork of any sort, no calendar, not even a coffee mug. Counters, cupboards, drawers, a sink, a dishwasher—it could have been a larger kitchen from the 1970s, except for the unusually deep refrigerators, two of them, one stacked on top of the other, with square doors.

In the centre of the room was a shiny metal table, on wheels, slightly inclined. It was covered in a sheet, the silhouette of which looked like a drawing a child might make of a mountain range, showing the peaks and valleys. Or like that illustration in *The Little Prince* of what appears to be a hat but is not a hat; it's actually a picture of a python that has swallowed an elephant.

The sheet, probably cotton, looked soft, and was pleasing in the muted warmth of its creamy colour. It was imprinted with a discrete pattern of crosshatched lines—I always have to check the spelling of that word, always mix them up, is it *discrete* or *discreet*? I got it wrong there, I mean discreet, as in quiet and unshowy, a pattern of pale grey lines, maybe an inch long, rounded at their ends, like caterpillars, set at right angles to each other, but not touching, creating the effect of a super-easy maze, perhaps a deliberate choice on the part of the funeral home, a breezy metaphor for dealing with death and grief. Don't worry, the loss of a loved one makes you feel like you're Theseus in the maze at Knossos, lost, but you'll find your way out, you will, don't worry—trust in the healing power of Ariadne.

Bryan delicately lifted a corner of the sheet from over the Minotaur, exposing your face and one shoulder, and laid it over your torso, a practiced move, it felt, like a bed being turned down for a guest at a luxury hotel. The fabric was heavy enough that it didn't need patting down, and the line of the fold ran neatly at an angle across your body, from just above one shoulder to the crook of your arm on the opposite side. I wondered: why this angle to the sheet, creating a triangle? Why not a rectangle, showing you as in a portrait? Perhaps because the size of the rectangle would have to be determined in the making of it, how much of the body to expose, it's hard to nail the golden ratio in one go, you don't want to be fiddling, whereas a triangle, once two points have been set—there was method in how Bryan pressed down on the fabric just off your right shoulder, then reached for the corner above your left shoulder—naturally falls into place, aim for a right-angle isosceles, just making sure the head is fully exposed: this much of the body will show, standard. If they want to see more, you can pull down the other corner, just make sure you lay the fabric down flat, people like neatness in these matters. But they won't want to see more, they never do.

The room, the sheet—details seared into my brain. That was grief for me at that moment: an eye that was furiously focused yet wandering. I noticed Bryan's ears, slightly red and nicely fleshy. Did his wife—he had a ring—like to nibble them when they made love? I felt shame; how could this thought enter my mind in the presence of your dead body?

"*War was back. War was running through the streets. War was entering every house.* **Hello! Hello!**" (55–56): Your face was bluish-grey and waxen, and sunken, the features somehow exaggerated. It had been nine months since I had seen you in person, but it looked like you, it was you—but as life-abandoned as a derelict prairie farmhouse, the doors broken, the windows shattered, whatever is left behind rusted or ravaged in its own way by the elements, brown the palette, a shell given over to the seasons, the human residents long gone. You had a coloured ribbon in your hair—I had the urge to pluck it out—and your hair looked like it had been brushed, but otherwise nothing cosmetic, and certainly nothing taxidermic, had been done to you, thank god. Embalming, what a job, what a barbarity. I flicked a look at Bryan. Why would you want your loved one's dead face puffed up, chemical pneumatics, Botox for those who are beyond vanity? Doesn't that make it even worse, garish falseness poorly concealing unavoidable truth, palimpsest as deceit?

The more I looked at your sweet little face, the more mottled your complexion appeared, and the less I saw my individual daughter and the more I beheld universal demise.

I gazed at your draped body. A child's body is small, by definition. It lay, you lay—which is it?—on a table meant to hold even the largest build. So much table, so little you. It looked terribly lonely. People crawl into hospital beds to be with their loved ones. But not here.

I recognized your long-sleeved T-shirt, a favourite of yours. Yellow, with some random colourful commercial logo, of which only a part showed from under the sheet. But weren't you wearing your pyjamas when you died? Yes, you were. You must have been changed into this T-shirt.

Your stillness was deeply jarring. That is death—not a smell, not a sight: stillness. You would never laugh again, you would never cry again, you would never wake up from this sleep, you would never grow up.

Gail spoke. "The funeral home gave us the winter storage rate. You know, for those who die in the middle of winter whose family want a spring burial because of the nicer weather. I got that rate, even though it was already spring, and now it's summer. Three hundred dollars. I thought it was a good deal."

"We call it *sheltering*," Bryan added. Another euphemism. He was just doing his job. He was trying to help. Shelter. From the storm. Why not? It did sound better. "And not here," he continued. "We sheltered her in a negative temperature unit. A quiet place."

"In other words, a freezer," said Gail. "It has been nine weeks and a day."

I was so tired, so desperately tired. How had it come to this?

"*War was back. War was running through the streets. War was entering every house.* **Hello! Hello!**" (80–81): My wife leaned over. "*Now* can we bury our daughter?" she hissed.

I looked at her, and all the demons came out. We had an argument, a verbal brawl like none I could have imagined. I can accept that a child might die, even that my child might die. Children die, in real life as well as in imagined worlds. In the Trojan War traditions, a daughter is sacrificed so that the war can take place. The founding act of Christianity is the death of a son as a son.

What I cannot accept is that over your corpse I had a fight with your mother, she on one side of you, I on the other, Bryan standing at your head. It was unholy. It was an obscenity.

Should Bryan have intervened, raising his hands, calling for peace? But that did not seem to be his inclination; he seemed to be shy and retiring by nature. Nor was it his role, professionally, to meddle, I'd think. People working in funeral homes are not there to rule or judge or enforce. They are passive receptacles of pain, like Hades, even misdirected pain. If you want to cry and wail, then cry and wail; we will provide tissues. If you want to faint, then faint; we will try to catch you. If you want to argue and shout, then argue and shout; we will get out of the way.

But this was something else. From our mouths spewed insults and accusations, foul language and hurtful words, barbs and jibes. In that mortuary, we rolled our eyes and laughed harshly, we yelled at the top of our voices. Bryan stood there, frozen, trying to be invisible, trying not to be there. Whenever I noticed him, he was looking elsewhere, mostly down, likely at you, perhaps at the maze covering you, trying to escape the real monsters in the room.

"Or did this terrible war wreck it all for her?" (104): "Get out! Get out! We're done. You're not spending another night in the house. You're moving out *today!*" Gail screamed.

She stormed out.

The mortuary was now quiet. I stood in a daze. I had failed. My life had come to this key moment, asking me to step up, to be, in a humble way, a hero, and I had failed. I had failed Gail, I had failed you. I apologized to you, kissing you on the forehead, and I apologized to Bryan. When I found my way back to where Gail had parked the car, the car was gone and my suitcases were lying on the ground. One had burst open. Amidst the colourful personal items—a sweater, T-shirts, some socks—I could make out a printout of *The Psoad*.

    I walked home.

Psoas Finds Prince Mestor's Residence

Psoas of Midea, the son of nobody,
who no longer had any fear of death
and so no love of life, walked through sacred Troy.
He pursued none, raised his sword against none.
He walked past the roaring and the shrieking,
he stepped over bodies and ignored the looters,
getting lost in the unfamiliar streets.
He was a sack of wheat loaded on a cart
that has torn and, unseen, slowly depletes
in a trickle of grain along the road. 10

He was an empty sack when at last we found
the residence of Prince Mestor, son of Priam
and Hecuba, brother of Hector and Paris,

besides many other brothers and sisters.

The place was bare and the spoils were meagre.
Expanses of marble and corners of dirt.
A household run by a broken widow.
In an inner room we found five bodies,
five starvelings, hanging from a beam by their necks.
The coldest, with a yellow face and blue lips,   20
was a small boy hanging high in the air,
curled like a hand of bananas on a hook.
Then came the bodies of a boy, a girl,
another boy, each a little older,
and finally the body of a woman,
lifeless and hollow-cheeked, her great beauty harried,
but her face still alive with wretchedness.

"*He was an empty sack*" (11): Shortly, I was summoned by my thesis supervisor.

"Hello, Gordon."

"Harlow, good to see you. Have a seat. Coffee? No? Okay. First off, I know you've been going through a tremendously hard time. My condolences about Helen. The news devastated Anne and me. It's an unspeakable loss. Please tell us when the funeral will be."

"I will. To be honest, I don't want to talk about it."

"Of course, of course. I'm sorry, I didn't mean to intrude. Well, in that case, moving on to other matters, I got a call from Franklin Cubitt. There was some confusion initially since he had your name wrong, but after that he was very clear. How did your work go at the Ancient World Library? I didn't hear as much about it as I thought I might. I figured you were busy. It's a rich trove, the Oxyrhynchus Papyri."

"The guy's a monster. He would scare Polyphemus."

"He has that reputation. But he does know his business and he was—how shall I put it?—uncertain about your academic contributions. You were supposed to parse the Greek-language Papyri to shed light on the social and economic lives of the citizens of Oxyrhynchus, is that right?"

"I did my best. His focus is very narrow. I took a broader approach, less literal, more interpretive."

"He found your methodology suspect. He used the word *balderdash*."

"If something explains, then how can it not be true? That's Homer, in essence."

"Right. Well, I should tell you that Cubitt compared what you did to the work of Dr. Frankenstein. A corpse with a thousand stitches, is how he put it. He also said your attendance at his weekly meetings was spotty. Apparently, you were travelling around Europe in the name of research, without his knowledge or approval, is that right? This was for your doctoral thesis, I presume. How is *Mutilations of the Corpse in* The Iliad coming along, by the way, speaking of corpses?"

"I want to talk to you about that. I've changed my topic."

"Have you?"

"Yes, I found something to say, as you told me to. That corpse."

"I see. But according to Cubitt, none of what that corpse has to say is suitable for publication. And I cannot convey to you how low in the estimation of Oxford's Faculty of Classics our small, fragile department has sunk. Cubitt also spoke to our president, who's never seen a budget he didn't want to slash. The ramifications, Harlow, the ramifications."

"The place was bare and the spoils were meagre" (15): I moved out to a dismal basement apartment, with yellowed walls and cramped windows that let in hardly any light. I was banished to Hades.

As a result of Cubitt's divine intervention, I was expelled from the doctoral program, my academic ambitions cancelled in one stroke. I am now like that scribe at the Mount Hymettos sanctuary to Zeus: I teach adults who are struggling with literacy.

"a small boy hanging high in the air, curled like a hand of bananas on a hook" (21–22): Surely the saddest reference to fruit in the literature of antiquity. It also serves as a useful date marker. The Mycenaeans did not know bananas. Bananas were brought to Asia Minor and Europe from India sometime in the fourth century BCE by Arab traders. So this striking comparison between the corpse of a little boy, yellowed by sadness and deprivation, reflexively curled despite the pull of the rope on his neck, and a cluster of bananas hanging from a hook is a late-added detail from classical Greek times, a fruit anachronism.

"her face still alive with wretchedness" (27): I have gone black, I who once was a chameleon, with only traces of colour when I close my eyes and imagine you in my arms.

Psoas Brings Hades the Flesh of Death

And so it was that Psoas of Midea,
the son of nobody, walked out of burning Troy,
Hermes guiding him, I at his side for a while,
the body of a small child in his arms,
he like a hand of bananas on a hook,
his only loot, and walked he to the Underworld,
summoned by the Lord of the Underworld,
arriving with no coinage, his eyes wide open,
to the unease of Charon, whose boat he rocked,
undead, the only living man in hell,   10
to the dread of Cerberus, whose bark the Lord stilled,
and settled he there, thick-bodied, next to Hades,
to whom he gave the small child. "Here, my lord,"
said he, "here is the flesh of death." Hades wept.

Through his tears the Lord of Death said, "I must die."
And still to this day, thick-bodied Psoas
dwells in the Underworld, next to Hades,
undead, the only living man in hell,
while I returned home to my wife and children.

"undead, the only living man in hell" (10): There it is, there it appears, from the fundament of ancient rumination—a living man in hell—and the longing for its symmetrical opposite. The central concept of Christianity, of a god who takes on death, must have come from somewhere. It could have come from the inventive Jews themselves, of course, but that would have required a vast conceptual leap, from a god who until then had made his cosmic infinity known only invisibly through a speaking fire, as with Moses, or in a whisper, as with Elijah, to an embodied god who walks, talks, suffers, and *dies*. Such an afflicted god is alien to Jews (as well as to Muslims and Hindus), but would have been familiar to the Ancient Greeks.

"Hades wept" (14)—a god who has been unmoved by countless deaths holds the body of a dead child in his arms and breaks down in tears. That is the flesh of death, then: how it feels. It was a mortal who had gone too far with his violence who taught an immortal that lesson, and that immortal never recovered. It was Hades, learning from Psoas of Midea, the son of nobody, who expressed the idea: "I must die" (15). He said it, and it was done. A Greek god was heard by a Jewish god, thanks to a Greek-speaking Jew, Paul of Tarsus, who wrote epistles about a Jewish messiah, the earliest texts of Christianity.

And so the conclusion: Jesus came from the incurable lassitude of a Greek soldier at Troy. From death eternal to life eternal. That is what you do with the sadness of mortals.

When I saw this fragment, which seems the logical end of *The Psoad*, a word jumped out from the very beginning of the epic, from the *Prologue*:

> Is he to *stay* in the gloom of Hades,
> nevermore to see the honey light of the world? (page 14, lines 2–3)

Psoas is still there, undead, the only living man in hell, just as Jesus is still there, living, the only dead god in heaven.

Troy: Jerusalem; Psoas: Jesus. Contrary complements. Stories that are at the start and heart of Western culture, our founding myths, the first, the oldest, offering redemption through poetry, the second, the latter, salvation by faith. For both, we have mere wisps of evidence, then stories, then the Greeks and the Christians. The creation is of the same form: wisps, stories, a people.

And so the conclusion: life is a walk, and while our bodies are solid, our joints are strong, and our vision is clear, yet we walk on feet of dreams.

"undead, the only living man in hell" (18): We never agreed on a funeral. You were cremated and your ashes were divided in two. You wander about forlornly, like the Ancient Greeks in the Underworld.

I can see you in the door frame, a shadow in pyjamas.
"Go back to bed, Helen," I tell you.
"No," you reply, with fierce conviction.
"It's late. You should be sleeping."
"Don't want to."
"You're tired."
"Am not."
"Do not come into the room, young lady."
"Tell me a story."
"I'm working."
"You're always working."
"No I'm not."
"Where's Mommy?" Your eyes are black holes that can never be filled.
"You know where Mommy is. You'll see her this weekend."
"Tell me a story."
"Go back to bed."
"I'm not going back to bed."
Silence.
"Just one story, *please*," you plead.
You always win. Does that make me a bad father?

"What story do you want?" I ask.
"The one about the broken pot."
"All right. Come sit here next to me."